Hail to the CHUMP

the misadventures of Willie Plummet

PAUL BUCHANAN
& ROD RANDALL

P9-CEU-458

CPH
SAINT LOUIS

The Misadventures of Willie Plummet

Invasion from Planet X
Submarine Sandwiched
Anything You Can Do I Can Do Better
Ballistic Bugs
Battle of the Bands
Gold Flakes for Breakfast
Tidal Wave
Shooting Stars
Hail to the Chump
The Monopoly

Cover illustration by John Ward.
Back cover photo by Ira Lippke.
Cover and interior design by Karol Bergdolt.

Scripture quotations taken from the HOLY BIBLE, NEW INTERNATIONAL VERSION®. NIV®. Copyright © 1973, 1978, 1984 by International Bible Society. Used by permission of Zondervan Publishing House. All rights reserved.

Copyright © 1998 Paul Buchanan
Published by Concordia Publishing House
3558 S. Jefferson Avenue, St. Louis, MO 63118-3968
Manufactured in the United States of America

Library of Congress Cataloging-in-Publication Data

Buchanan, Paul, 1959-
  Hail to the chump / Paul Buchanan & Rod Randall.
      p.   cm. — (The misadventures of Willie Plummet)
  Summary: Willie Plummet, who has a talent for misadventure, discovers how his Christian values apply to politics when he becomes entangled in the election for president of his eighth-grade class.
    ISBN 0-570-05088-X
    [1. Elections—Fiction.   2. Politics, Practical—Fiction. 3. Christian life—Fiction.]
  I. Randal, Rod, 1962-   . II. Title. III. Series: Buchanan, Paul, 1959-   Misadventures of Willie Plummet.
  PZ7.B87717Hai   1998
  [Fic]—dc21   98-19605
                                                                   AC

2   3   4   5   6   7   8   9   10   07   06   05   04   03   02   01   00   99   98

For Mitch and Max

Contents

① Can You Keep a Secrete?

"Harriet *Bink?*" Felix sputtered. "Harriet Bink for class *president?*" He couldn't believe what he was reading. He sat across the table from me, looking up at the poster on the cafeteria wall. He shook his head. "I don't think she'd even vote for herself." He picked up his slice of pizza and crammed the pointed end in his mouth. I popped open the can of juice that came with my lunch and took a sip.

Harriet Bink for president. It *did* seem a little odd. Harriet was not a popular girl. It wasn't that people disliked her; it was just that she didn't go out of her way to make friends. She was always serious—a straight-A student, captain of the debate team. It was almost like she was an adult. When you were around her you felt like you should behave. She was the last person anyone would vote for.

I swiveled around on my chair and looked up at the red, white, and blue banner: **ELECT HARRIET BINK CLASS PRESIDENT.**

"Maybe it's some kind of joke," I said.

Felix shook his head and pointed his half-eaten slice of pizza toward the front of the cafeteria. "She's sitting right over there," he said with his mouth full. "She would have torn it down by now if it was a joke."

I looked at Harriet. She was eating lunch with some other girls. She had a napkin on her lap and was eating a slice of pepperoni pizza with a knife and fork. I looked back at Felix. Pizza grease dribbled down his chin. A spot of red pizza sauce dotted his cheek.

"I'll bet she eats all four basic food groups at each meal," Felix said. "And she probably chews 32 times before swallowing."

"Harriet's not that bad," I told him. "She's just a little too serious. Now will you wipe off your face? You've got stuff all over it."

"Harriet doesn't have a chance of being elected," Felix said. "She never smiles." Felix dabbed his chin with a paper napkin. "Harriet's just not popular enough to be president."

"It's not supposed to be a popularity contest," I told him. "It's supposed to be about qualifications and ideas. She might get some votes." Deep down, though, I had to admit it did seem unlikely.

Felix shook his head. "If the *teachers* could vote, she'd be elected Grand Emperor of Glenfield or something," Felix said. "But what kid's going to vote for Harriet Bink?"

"*I* might vote for her," Sam said as she put her tray down next to Felix's, dropped her backpack on the floor, and sat down in the seat we'd saved for her. Sam bowed her head for a moment to say grace.

Sam, Felix, and I always eat lunch together. We are a team, best friends really. The three of us are always working on some project together—like the Video Sub or the Skyrunner 1000. We have quite a reputation in Glenfield as inventors.

Sam sat down and tucked her blonde hair behind her ears. "But my vote would depend on who the other two candidates were," she said.

At Glenfield Middle School there could be only three candidates for any elected office—don't ask me why. It had been like that for years.

"*You'd* vote for Harriet Bink?" Felix asked. "Tell me it isn't so. If she were class president, she'd want to extend the school year."

"I know she's wound a little tight," Sam admitted. "But she's smart and responsible. She's got some good ideas. I can think of kids who'd make worse presidents."

"Yeah?" Felix said skeptically. "Like who? Harriet would be the last person I'd ever vote for."

Sam shook her head. "She wouldn't be the *last* person you'd vote for."

"Absolute dead last," Felix insisted.

Sam fixed her eyes on him. "Okay, smart guy. Who would you vote for: Harriet Bink or Leonard Grubb?"

Felix squirmed. Sam had him there. Leonard "the Crusher" Grubb was the school bully. He'd probably shoved, insulted, and terrorized every person—including me—in this crowded cafeteria. He devoted himself heart and soul to the craft of bullying. It was his calling in life. Felix glanced around the cafeteria to see where Leonard was before he answered.

Leonard Grubb sat by himself three tables away. He held an aluminum can upside down and shook the last few drops of grape juice into his open mouth. When he noticed us all looking at him, he grinned and crushed the can against his forehead.

"Who is he trying to impress?" Sam asked.

"Okay," Felix admitted, "I'd vote for Harriet. But Crusher Grubb isn't going to run for class president. You haven't proven anything."

"Felix is right," I told Sam. "Harriet hasn't got a chance. Any of us could beat her in an election."

"Yeah," Felix said. "Maybe I'll run against her."

"Don't flatter yourself, Felix," Sam said. "You and Harriet would split the nerd vote, and the other candidate would walk away with the election."

"Oh yeah?" Felix sputtered, pulling back the tab on his can of juice. "I'd do a lot better than that. I think I'd get the whole nerd vote by myself. I'd leave Harriet in the dust."

"Will you *listen* to yourself?" I told Felix. "This is an argument you're not going to win." Felix is my best friend, not a nerd. But he's smart enough to be one.

Felix sighed and took a gulp of juice.

"I'm serious," Sam said. "Harriet has some good ideas. Did you guys see the pamphlet she's passing out? She gave me one in social studies."

Felix and I both shook our heads. Sam bent and unzipped her backpack. "She's probably only giving them to people she thinks can read," Sam said with a grin. She rummaged through her backpack. "Harriet thinks we need to expand the library," Sam said. "She also thinks the eighth-grade field trip shouldn't have been canceled."

"Well, who doesn't?" Felix snorted. "But is Harriet going to pay for it?"

Every year the eighth-graders took an all-day field trip to the Cedarville Observatory before Christmas break. It was a tradition, but now that it was our turn, the trip had been canceled. The school didn't have the money to pay for our transportation and admission. We all felt cheated.

Sam was still looking through her backpack for Harriet's brochure. "What's *this*?" she asked.

Sam straightened up. She held a light blue envelope in her hand. It looked like a greeting card. "*Samantha*," she read out loud from the front of the envelope. "Nobody calls me Samantha." She put her thumb under the flap and tore the envelope open. The card she pulled out had a bouquet of red roses in the shape of a heart on the front. Sam's brow furrowed. She opened the card. As she read, a smile spread across her face.

Sam closed the card and slapped it down on the table. "Very funny," she said, grinning. "Which of you two spazzes pulled this one?"

I had no idea what she was talking about. I looked at Felix. He shrugged.

"You guys didn't think I'd actually fall for this, did you?" Sam asked. "It's the oldest practical joke in the book."

I picked up the card and opened it. I angled it so Felix and I could read it at the same time. Printed inside the card was a poem. Felix read it aloud.

> It isn't just the way you smile
> Or the gracious things you do.
> I love you for the way I feel
> Each time I think of you.

Felix made a face like he'd just bit into a lemon.

Beneath the poem, the card was signed in blue pen, "*A Secrete Admirer.*"

"Give us some credit," I told Sam. "Felix and I are both smart enough to know the difference between *secret* and *secrete.*"

"Yeah," she said. "And you're both smart enough to use the wrong word on purpose so I wouldn't think one of you sent this thing."

She was right—and it was kind of flattering.

"It wasn't me," I told her truthfully. I closed the card and slid it across the table to her.

"Me neither," Felix said.

Sam looked from me to Felix and back again. "*Promise?*" she asked.

Felix raised his hand like he was being sworn into office. "I promise," he told her.

Sam looked me in the eye. "Me too," I told her. "It looks like you've got a genuine *secrete* admirer."

Sam's brow furrowed again. She looked around at the kids talking and laughing at the crowded cafeteria tables. I knew what she was thinking: Any one of the boys could have slipped that card into her backpack. She sighed. "*Please* don't tell anyone about this," she whispered. "It would be too embarrassing."

"Your secretion is safe with us," I told her.

2

Do You Wuv Me?

I was walking up the steps to my front door when I heard a voice.

"Willie, *dah*ling," the voice said with some kind of lah-de-dah accent. "The fates have brought you here to admire my artwork."

"Huh?"

"Come over here and see what I'm working on, you big dope," the voice told me in a suddenly normal voice.

I groaned. It was Phoebe, my 9-year-old next-door neighbor. She was in her garage with the door open. I couldn't see her, but I knew she was up to something lame. Phoebe's actually pretty cool—she's really smart and she's gotten me out of more than a few sticky situations—but she's had a crush on me since she was born. Sometimes it's embarrassing.

"I'm kind of busy right now," I said to her, my hand on our front doorknob. "I've got to help Sadie with her math homework."

Phoebe peeked around the edge of her open garage door. "Sadie is a *dog*," she pointed out. "She's a cocker spaniel."

"I know," I said. "That's why she needs so much help with long division."

Phoebe stepped all the way out of the garage and put her hands on her hips. "If I didn't know better, I'd think you were avoiding me."

I sighed. "Okay," I said. "What is it you want to show me?"

"My mural," she said.

"Your mural?"

"Yeah," she said. "That's when you paint a picture on a wall."

"I *know* what a mural is," I told her. "I just didn't know you were painting one."

"Dad said I could," Phoebe told me. "It's going up on my bedroom wall. I'm working on some sketches now. Come see."

I reluctantly followed Phoebe into her garage. There was a huge partially unrolled roll of butcher paper on the floor. Pens and pencils, markers and paintbrushes were scattered around the huge sheet of paper on the concrete floor. Phoebe had all kinds of art supplies—she's a good artist for a little kid.

Phoebe stood over the butcher paper. "What do you think?" she asked. "This is the actual size." I looked down at the huge picture unrolled on the garage floor. It took a moment for my eyes to adjust to the dim light in the garage. "I call it 'Prince Charming,'" Phoebe said.

There on the paper was a princess dressed in pink, wearing one of those pointy, cone-shaped princess hats. In front of her, down on one knee as if he were proposing, was the prince. He was holding the girl's hand like he was about to kiss it. Behind them in the distance was a castle, high on a hill. As my eyes adjusted to the light, I looked again at the princess. She looked amazingly like Phoebe, only older—and prettier.

"Wow," I said. "You're really good. That princess looks just like you."

Phoebe laughed nervously. It was then that it dawned on me.

I stepped closer to the picture and stared down at the face of Prince Charming.

"No!" I shouted. "You can't *do* that."

"Do what?" Phoebe asked, trying to sound innocent.

"Your Prince Charming looks just like me."

"Does it?" Phoebe asked. "I hadn't noticed."

"You're *not* painting that on your bedroom wall," I shouted. "I'll sue."

"Come on, Willie. No one will see it," Phoebe pleaded. "It'll just be in my room."

"Are you kidding?" I said. "Everytime you have one of your dumb slumber parties, all your little friends will see it. It'll be all over town."

"I don't have slumber parties," Phoebe said. "And if I did, we'd all sleep in the living room."

"I don't care," I told her. "You're not painting my face on your bedroom wall."

"You can't really sue me," Phoebe pointed out. "I can paint it on my wall if I want."

"You put me on your wall and I'll never talk to you again," I threatened.

Phoebe looked crestfallen. She knew I was serious.

"Okay," she said. "You win."

I was still fuming at Phoebe when I stepped into my bedroom. *Prince Charming*? Where does she get off?

After dinner I decided to work on my math homework in the living room. It was a pretty dumb assignment. We were supposed to find a bunch of points on a sheet of graph paper, then connect them to make a picture—a fancy kind of connect the dots. It was dull, tedious work that didn't require a lot of attention, so I thought I'd do it in the living room while Dad watched the news on TV.

I found about a hundred points on the graph and connected them with straight lines. So far all I had was a crazy line that zigzagged across the graph paper. I had no idea what the picture was supposed to be. I began to wonder if I was doing it right.

I picked up the phone to call Felix. He had the same assignment. I thought maybe if he'd already finished the picture, he could tell me if I was on the right track. When I put the phone to my ear, I heard voices.

"I wuv ooo too, sweetie."

"Not as much as me wuvs ooo."

It was my older sister, Amanda, and her boyfriend, Darryl, cooing to each other in baby talk. It made me want to hurl.

"Wait a minute!" my sister's voice snarled suddenly. "Did someone just pick up the phone? Who's listening in? I can hear a television set somewhere."

"Me just picked up the phone to tell ooo two it's time for beddy-bye," I said in my best baby voice.

"Is that you, Willie?" Amanda shouted into the phone. "This is a private conversation! Get off the phone!"

"Sounds like someone needs a nap," I told her.

"Willie," Amanda threatened. "If you don't hang up right now, I'm coming downstairs to tell Dad you're listening in again."

"I'm not listening in," I told them. "If I wanted to listen to nauseating baby talk, I'd work in the church nursery more often. But I need to make a call. When will you two be done doing whatever this is you're doing?"

"When we're good and ready," Amanda told me. "Now hang up, you little creep."

"Gladly," I said. I stuck my tongue out at the telephone receiver, then hung it up and went back to my homework. I worked for a few more minutes, but the picture still didn't seem to be taking shape. I thought about trying to call Felix again, but there was no way I would run the risk of hearing more baby talk. I just kept connecting dots.

After a while my hand started cramping. I opened and closed it a few times. I glanced at the news on the television while I rubbed my sore palm. The president was descending the steps of Air Force One, waving. Hundreds of flashbulbs were going off and a band was playing "Hail to the Chief." The image shifted to the president standing behind a podium indoors. The presidential seal—that blue circle with the eagle in the middle—decorated the front of the podium. The president was giving some sort of speech. More flashbulbs went off.

I thought about how the president appeared on millions of television sets around the world every day. I mean, imagine all the fame and respect that comes with being president. Everyone in the world knows who you are. Everywhere you go, crowds gather. Think of all the monuments and awards and honors you can get. You can even end up with your face on a postage stamp or on Mount Rushmore or on a hundred dollar bill.

I looked down at my homework. Suddenly I saw what the picture was going to be—it was the same eagle that appeared on the president's seal. *Wow*, I thought, *what a weird coincidence*.

I looked back up at the television, but a dog food commercial was on now. An Irish setter was wolfing down chunks of brown meat that had just been dumped into a blue dish. I glanced over at Dad, hoping it didn't remind him of a certain chili incident. But he was just sitting there in his recliner, watching.

Then the television hissed, and the picture wobbled a little. Everything changed color for a few seconds, then the picture returned to normal.

Dad leaped out of his chair. "Did you see that?" he asked, full of excitement. "The television's broken!"

"No, it isn't, Dad," I said quickly. "It was just the antenna or something. Look. It's fine now."

Dad was taking an electronics class at Glenfield Community College. For weeks he'd been scrounging around for broken electrical appliances to take to his class. He'd already fixed everything in the house—some things twice. Now he was getting desperate for something to break. He did good work, but he took his time. If he took the television, it might be gone for weeks.

"See?" I said after a few seconds. "Everything's fine."

"*Now* it is," Dad said. "But a minute ago the picture was jumping all over the place. Maybe I should take it into the shop to do some bench tests—just to be sure."

I ransacked my mind for way to stop him. "The television seems to be working fine now, Dad," I said again. "But between you and me, there's been a weird humming noise on the telephone in Amanda's room for a couple of weeks now."

"Hmmm," Dad said, obviously pleased with the news. "I think I'd better have a look at it." Dad went into the kitchen where he'd left his toolbox, then headed up the stairs toward Amanda's room.

I smiled. "That's what *ooo* gets for being a *cwanky* sister," I said aloud in a baby voice.

～⌒～⌒

That night in bed, I read Philippians 1. The youth pastor at my church had challenged us to read a chapter of the Bible each night. After I finished reading, I rolled over, turned off the light, and closed my eyes. I kept thinking about the eagle picture I'd done for math and how it looked just like the presidential seal.

I thought about Harriet Bink running for class president and how Felix had said anyone could beat her. I thought about what it would be like to be class president. Maybe it would be the first step of a journey that would take me to the White House. As I drifted off to sleep, I imagined a fifth face on Mount Rushmore—one belonging to 13-year-old Willie Plummet.

How Do You Get the Rabbit to Sit Still?

The next day at lunch, I found an empty table and sat down with my tray. In a few minutes, Sam came in and joined the end of the lunch line. Felix was nowhere in sight.

Sam brought her tray over and sat down across from me. She bowed her head and said a quick prayer before lifting her fork.

"Where's Felix?" I asked her. "I haven't seen him all day."

"He's in Mr. Keefer's class working on a lab project," she told me. "Mr. Keefer's letting him work an extra hour because he didn't get it done by the end of the period."

"*Felix?*" I said. "Mr. Science didn't get his lab project done? How did that happen?"

"Todd Larson is his lab partner," Sam explained. "But he's out with the flu. Felix got paired with Leonard Grubb for the day."

"Poor Felix," I said, shaking my head.

"Leonard, of course, didn't lift a finger," Sam went on. "And Felix was so nervous, he kept knocking everything over. So he's spending the lunch hour redoing the whole project. You know how Felix is about grades."

"Yeah," I laughed. "And this could be the first time Leonard Grubb will get an A on anything."

Suddenly an orange flew through the air behind Sam. A few seconds later a fudge brownie flew back the other way.

"Uh-oh," I said. "Looks like a food fight."

Sam looked over her shoulder. A hamburger bun sailed through the air like a Frisbee.

"All right, who started this?" a deep voice demanded. It was Mr. Frieze, the history teacher. It was his turn for cafeteria duty. He stood at the front of the room, looking out over all the tables. "Who's responsible for this juvenile behavior?"

Everyone fell silent. No one said a word. We just looked at Mr. Frieze. It seemed like all of us were holding our breath.

A few tables away, Harriet Bink rose to her feet. "I saw the whole thing," she said loudly and clearly. "It was Jesse Ingraffia and Patrick Connolly." She sat back down.

My mouth fell open. *What was she thinking*? She was running for president and she had the gall to stand up in front of everyone and rat on two of her peers. The whole cafeteria stared at Harriet in shocked silence. It was clear she'd lost more than just Jesse's and Patrick's votes.

"Ingraffia, Connolly—come with me," Mr. Frieze demanded. The two boys rose from their seats and shuffled nervously to the front. They followed Mr. Frieze out of the cafeteria.

Even after they were gone, the cafeteria remained strangely silent. Everyone talked in whispers. I looked up on the wall at Harriet Bink's banner. As I was looking at it, someone spattered it with ketchup.

By fifth period, I had made up my mind: I was definitely going to run for president. It seemed to be my destiny. There was no way Harriet could beat me, especially after today's episode in the cafeteria. I knew this whole thing wasn't supposed to be a popularity contest, but I was more popular than Harriet and that couldn't hurt.

When the bell rang to end fifth period, I tore a couple of sheets of paper from my three-ring binder. As everyone filed out of class, I sat at my desk scribbling. I wrote the same note on both sheets:

Meet me at the lab at four.
I've got something important to tell you.

Willie

I folded each sheet three times. When I left the classroom, people already were coming in for the next class. I went to Felix's locker first and slid one of the notes through the vent slots. Then I headed down the hall toward Sam's locker. The halls already had emptied—I'd have to hurry to make it to my next class on time.

I turned the corner. Leonard Grubb was leaning against the wall directly across from Sam's locker. I ducked back around the corner and peeked at him. He was just standing there. No one else was around. I watched him for a few seconds, but he didn't seem to be going anywhere or doing anything. He was just leaning against the wall, staring down at the floor tiles. *Great*, I thought. *Not only will I be late to class, but I won't be able to leave a note for Sam.*

Just as I was about to give up and head to class, Leonard moved down the hall and bent over the drinking fountain. His back was turned to me. I might have just enough time.

I slid up to Sam's locker like a ninja and slipped the note through the vent slot. I was back around the corner before Leonard knew a thing.

That afternoon I sat at my workbench at the lab, which is really the storeroom at the back of my family's hobby shop. It's the place where Felix, Sam, and I have created our greatest inventions. I was doodling with red and blue felt-tip pens on a pad of paper, trying to design a poster to announce my candidacy for class president. **VOTE FOR WILLIE!** one version read. **PLUMMET FOR PRESIDENT!** read another. They looked okay, but I needed to think of something a bit more original—something that would get more attention than Harriet's posters.

A few minutes before four, someone banged on the back door. I got up from the workbench and pulled the door open. Sam and Felix stood in the alleyway. Sam looked mad.

"Dude," Felix said, laughing, "she got another one."

"Shut up, Felix," Sam said. She pushed Felix aside and walked through the door. She went over to the workbench and plopped down on my stool with her arms crossed. Normally, I'd have asked her for my seat back, but she looked like she might bite my head off.

"What did you *do* to her?" I whispered to Felix. "I don't think I've ever seen her this mad." Felix pulled the door shut behind him.

"Me?" he asked. "I didn't do a thing. It was the Secret Secreter."

"Huh?"

"The guy," Felix said. "Sam's secret admirer. He struck again. He slipped a note into her locker through the air vents." Felix glanced around the lab as if he were looking for something. "Let's go get something to eat," he said. "I didn't have any lunch."

Sam was still sitting in a huff on my stool with her arms crossed. When I looked at her, she looked away.

"You've got to see it," Felix said. "He wrote another poem. It's hilarious."

I looked over at Sam.

"There's no way I'm going to show it to you," Sam said. "For all I know, *you're* the one who sent it. I wouldn't put it past you to think this was funny."

"It wasn't me," I said. "I promise. Come on, let me see it. Maybe I can help you figure out who sent it."

Sam groaned and raised up on the stool enough to pull the note from a back pocket of her jeans. She held it out to me. I took it, but Felix snatched it from my grip.

"Let me read it out loud," Felix said. "This is rich." He cleared his throat and began reading aloud while I looked over his shoulder.

Little birds fly through the air.
I like the way you comb your hare.
You are as pretty as a pearl.
I wish that you would be my girl (friend).

I tried my hardest not to laugh, but it was impossible. Felix started laughing too. He could barely finish reading the pitiful thing. Sam just sat scowling at both of us.

"It's kind of touching," I said, once I regained my composure. "But I didn't know you had a rabbit."

Felix busted up laughing again, then I did too.

"Shut up, both of you," Sam said. She leaned over and snatched the note from Felix's hand. She stuffed it back in her pocket.

"What's *with* you?" I asked Sam. "You should be flattered. Some guy's got a crush on you. That's a *good* thing."

Sam glared at me. "Look who's talking," she said. "You've been complaining your whole life because the girl next door has a crush on you."

I thought about the Prince Charming picture in Phoebe's garage and winced.

"That's different," I told her.

"No, it isn't," Sam said. "It's exactly the same thing."

"It's different," I insisted. "Phoebe's a little kid. At least *your* admirer is close to your own age. *He* isn't going to invite you to a birthday party at a Chuck E. Cheese."

"Pizza sounds good," Felix said. "Let's go get some pizza." We both ignored him.

"But mine's a *secret* admirer," Sam said.

"You mean a *secrete* admirer," Felix said with a laugh. Sam glared at him. He stopped laughing and stepped behind me.

"At least *you* know who your admirer is," Sam said to me. "Mine's sneaking around like some kind of stalker."

"Maybe he's just shy," I said. "Maybe he's the strong silent type." Felix came out from behind me and took the pad of paper I'd been doodling on from the workbench.

"How am I supposed to feel?" Sam asked. "Some guy likes me, but he's such a cream puff, he's too scared to talk to me."

"Mmmmm. Cream puffs," Felix said looking up from the pad of paper. "I could go for a couple of those right now. Let's go to the donut shop." We both ignored him again.

"It's just annoying," Sam said. "I don't have time for a secret admirer."

"Just relax," I told her. "This is nothing to be upset about. Ignore it for now. I'm sure you'll find out who he is sooner or later."

"Say, what is this stuff?" Felix asked. He was staring down at my pad of paper with all the doodles on it. This wasn't how I'd planned to make my announcement.

"Give me that." I snatched the pad of paper from Felix's hands. "You weren't supposed to look at that."

"What is it?" Sam asked.

"This is why I called this meeting," I said. "I didn't call you here to talk about secret admirers. I have an announcement to make. I've decided to run for class president."

"Cool," Felix said. He looked around the lab again. "Didn't you have a box of Twinkies in here last week?"

Sam sat on my stool with her arms crossed, still a bit ticked. I don't know what reaction I expected from them—but this wasn't it. I hadn't expected them to carry me from the lab on their shoulders, but I thought they'd at least show some enthusiasm.

"Hel-*lo*?" I said. "Hel-*lo*. Have I turned invisible, or did you both go deaf? Did you hear what I just said?"

"Yeah. Sure. Running for president," Felix said, still looking around. "You didn't eat all those Twinkies yourself, did you?"

"Look, will you two stop thinking of yourselves for a minute here?" I said. "Will you get your minds off Twinkies and your stupid secret admirer? I just told you I'm running for president. As my best friends, you two should be a bit more supportive."

Sam and Felix looked at each other.

"You're right," Sam said. "I think it's a great idea. If you win, you'll make a wonderful president."

"What do you mean, *if* I win? Remember, I'm running against Harriet Bink."

"Harriet might be a lot tougher to beat than you think," Sam said. "She's smart, and she's on the debate team—and there's also room for one more person on the ballot. It could end up being anyone. You might be able to beat Harriet—but what if the other person on the ballot is Amy McDonald?"

"*McDonald's*?" Felix said. "Let's go get some hamburgers." We ignored him.

"I'm pretty sure I can win," I told Sam.

"If you win, will you try to get our field trip to the Cedarville Observatory back?" Felix asked.

"I'll try," I said. "But first I have to get elected. I'll need your help. I want one of you to be my campaign manager."

Sam and Felix looked at each other.

"Who?" Felix asked. "Who do you want? I'd be great."

"Hold on there, sport," Sam said. "I'd be just as good. Who did you have in mind, Willie?"

"I don't know," I said. "I thought I'd let you guys decide between yourselves."

"How about we both make up a campaign slogan?" Sam suggested. "The best slogan wins."

"You're on," Felix said.

"You guys think you can come up with some slogans by tomorrow morning?" I asked. "I'd like to get my poster up in the cafeteria as soon as possible."

"What do you say, Felix?" Sam teased. "You willing to give up looking through your telescope for one night?"

"Sure thing," Felix said. "You willing to give up combing your rabbit?"

④

Willie Win?

I met Sam and Felix the next morning at the flagpole. When Felix saw me coming, he could hardly contain his excitement.

"You've got to see it, dude," he told me. "This slogan is going to win you the election."

He handed me the pad of paper. There in neat letters was Felix's slogan:

> Pb might PLUMMET
> But WILLIE'S as good as Au

I had no idea what it meant. I glanced at Sam. She shrugged.

"Don't you *get* it?" Felix asked. "You know—it's the chemical symbols for lead and gold."

I read it again. It still didn't make sense.

"You know," Felix said, a note of desperation in his voice. "Lead's heavy—it *plummets* when you drop it."

I read it a third time. I didn't know what to say. It was the worst campaign slogan I'd ever read.

"It's not exactly catchy," Sam pointed out.

"Oh, yeah?" Felix asked. "I'd like to see you do better."

"As a matter of fact, I did," Sam said. She pulled a folded sheet of paper from her math book and handed it to Felix.

Felix opened it and read it aloud.

WILLIE WIN?
Only if you vote!
PLUMMET FOR PRESIDENT

"I believe we have a winner," I said.

"You think *that's* better than mine?" Felix sputtered. "You can't be serious."

"Yes, it's better," Sam said. "And I'm the campaign manager. The judge's decision is final."

"Well, if she's your stupid campaign manager, what am I supposed to do?" Felix asked. "What's my job?"

"I don't know," I told him. "You can do a lot of things—odds and ends. You can write speeches and help plan strategy. You're still an important part of my campaign. You can do anything you want."

"How about I be your bodyguard?" Felix suggested. "I've got a pair of dark glasses."

"What do I need a bodyguard for?" I asked. "Besides, I'm bigger than you are."

"He can always throw himself in front of a flying fudge brownie if another food fight breaks out in the cafeteria," Sam said.

"Ha, ha, ha!" Felix said.

"Look, Felix, I have to get a hundred signatures to get my name on the ballot," I told him. "That's something you can work on. See if you can get all the signatures today so we can turn them in to the school office tomorrow morning."

"Okay," Felix said. "I can do that."

"We also have to get some big paper so I can make our campaign poster," Sam said.

"*You're* going to make it?" Felix snickered. "Your handwriting is even worse than mine. If you paint the banner, it's going to look like a doctor's prescription."

Sam sighed. "You're right," she admitted. "We're only allowed one poster—it's got to look great. None of us has the artistic talent to pull it off."

"So we need some big paper *and* someone with artistic talent," Felix said. "Any ideas, Willie?"

"Yeah," I said. "I know someone who has both."

"I'll do it," Phoebe said. She sat on her front steps, looking up at me. "But on one condition."

I didn't like the sound of this. I wasn't very good with conditions—I'm not a good haggler. "What condition?" I asked.

"You give me permission to proceed with my mural."

"Phoebe!"

"The mural or no deal," she said. "You need a banner. I've got the paper. I've got the talent. I'm the woman for the job."

I groaned. My mind raced, trying to think of a compromise. But like I said, I'm lousy at haggling. "Look, the painting is Prince Charming, right?" I reasoned. "How about you paint him in full armor, with one of those visors over his face? Then no one will know it's me."

"No deal," Phoebe said. She thought for a moment. "I am willing to give him a mustache."

"A beard," I said. "And I mean a *full beard*—I'm talking Santa Claus."

"A goatee," Phoebe said. "A cute pointy one. That and a mustache."

I sighed. "Okay," I said. "It's a deal."

"Your banner will be ready in the morning before school starts."

Amanda spent most of the evening in the kitchen on the phone, talking to her boyfriend. Now that Dad had taken her telephone to his electronics class, she almost lived in the kitchen. I sat in the living room while Dad watched the news. Every few seconds, I'd hear the annoying fake laugh Amanda uses when she's talking to a boy on the phone.

I was done with my homework. All I had to do now was call Felix to make sure he'd gotten all the necessary signatures to put my name on the ballot. It wasn't that I didn't trust him. It's just that he'd gotten us all in a heap of trouble once when he'd tried to register our rock band for a contest—but that's another story.

Anyway, Amanda had been talking on the phone for at least an hour. I was getting impatient. I got up off the sofa and went into the kitchen. Amanda was sitting at the kitchen table.

When I came through the swinging kitchen door, Amanda stopped baby talking and said, "Hold on, my brother just came in." She covered the phone's mouthpiece with her hand. "What do you want?" she snarled.

"Me just wants some milk," I said in a baby voice.

I ducked under the stretched phone cord and went to the refrigerator. I poured myself a glass of milk. Amanda waited with her hand over the phone's mouthpiece. I closed the refrigerator door and pulled out a chair at the kitchen table.

"What do you think you're doing?" Amanda asked.

I sat down. "Just enjoying a refreshing and nutritious glass of milk," I said. I raised the glass to Amanda in a toast, then took a sip.

"Get out of here," she snarled.

"I'm not done with my milk yet," I told her. I took another small sip and dabbed the corners of my mouth with a fingertip.

"I'm having a conversation here," Amanda growled.

"Don't let me stop you." I took another tiny sip, just to show I'd be parked for a while.

"Get lost, you little creep," she said. She wasn't just covering the mouthpiece now, she was strangling it.

"This is the kitchen," I said. "This isn't your bedroom. I have as much right to be here as you do."

Amanda glared at me. She uncovered the mouthpiece of the phone. "Darryl?" she said in a singsong voice. "Can I call you right back? I need to move to another extension."

She glared at me again. "I wuv ooo too," she said into the phone before she hung up and stomped out of the kitchen.

I picked up the phone before the kitchen door stopped swinging. It was still warm. I dialed Felix's number.

"You're in, dude," Felix told me when his mom gave him the phone. "It was easy—I had a hundred signatures before fourth period. I've got the petition right here. Everybody wanted to sign it. You're going to win this election by a landslide."

"This isn't supposed to be a popularity contest," I reminded him. "I don't want to be elected just because people like me. I want to be elected because I have good ideas."

Just then there was a clicking noise on the phone and the tones of someone dialing a number.

"Shhhhh," I told Felix.

I waited a couple of seconds, then said "Hello" in a deep voice, like I had just answered the phone.

"Darryl?" Amanda asked. "Sorry about that, my dumb brother came into the kitchen, and I couldn't talk."

"You really shouldn't call your brother dumb," I said, still using the deep voice.

"Huh?" Amanda said. "Darryl?"

"From what I can see, he's a brilliant, strapping young man."

"Who is this?" Amanda demanded.

"He's also quite good-looking," I added.

"Willie?" Amanda said. "Will you get off the phone! I'm talking to Darryl. Stop listening in."

"You're not talking to Darryl," I pointed out. "*I'm* talking to *Felix*."

"Huh?"

"Hi, Amanda," Felix said. "How's it going?"

"You know, I really don't appreciate you listening in on us," I told Amanda. "This is a private conversation."

"Okay, you little creep, finish your conversation and get off the phone," Amanda told me.

"Sure thing," I said. "Felix, you told me you got a hundred signatures on the petition. Could you read them to me?"

"Sure," Felix said and started reading slowly. "Nikki Adams, Tim Watkins, Mitch Reynolds ..."

Amanda groaned and hung up.

Where Did I Leave My Purse?

I got ready for bed and turned on my bedside lamp. I opened my Bible to Philippians 2 and started to read.

> *Do nothing out of selfish ambition or vain conceit, but in humility consider others better than yourselves. Each of you should look not only to your own interests, but also to the interests of others.*

Those two verses struck me as important. I underlined them with my pencil. It seemed to me that there was a lot being said in those verses, and I wanted to come back to them and think about them.

I read through to the end of the chapter, then I went back and looked at those two verses. "In humility consider others better than yourselves," I read out loud. I looked at the next verse. "Your attitude should be the same as that of Jesus Christ," I said.

I thought about how I'd treated Amanda earlier that night. I'd wanted to get even with her for tying up the phone. But would I have done that if I really considered her *better than me*? I thought about Harriet, and how I thought I was better than her because I was more popular. Was that *vain conceit*?

I rolled over and switched off the bedside light. I was still thinking about those two verses when I asked Jesus to help me have an attitude like His and fell asleep.

When I woke up, it was light outside. My clock radio hadn't come on yet, but it looked too bright to be before six in the morning. I rolled over to check the time. My clock was gone. I sat bolt upright. I jumped out of bed and grabbed my watch from the dresser. It was 7:30! I was going to be late for school.

I got dressed, brushed my teeth, and dashed downstairs. I wouldn't have time for breakfast. I ran into the kitchen where Amanda and Orville were eating cereal.

"Who stole my alarm clock?" I shouted. "I'm going to be late for school."

"Dad took it," Orville told me. "He just left with it."

"Dad?" I asked. "Why?"

"I might have mentioned that it wasn't working properly," Amanda said. "I'm sure you'll get it back in a week or so." She gave me her most annoying grin.

I was ready to yell at her when I remembered the verses I'd read the night before. I guess I deserved it. I grabbed a donut and headed next door.

When I rang Phoebe's doorbell, the door swung open immediately. Phoebe stood there, holding a large cardboard tube.

"I've been waiting for you, Willie," she said, holding out the tube. "You're late."

"I know. I know."

"I worked on this all last night," she said.

I took the tube.

"Tonight, I'll start the mural," she added. I winced.

"Thanks, Phoeb," I told her. "You're a lifesaver."

"Don't you want to look at it?" she asked.

"No time," I told her. "You didn't misspell any of the words, did you?"

Phoebe put her hands on her hips and tried to look offended. "How can you ask me that?" she said. "Remember, last year I was—"

"Sixteenth place in the state spelling bee championship," I finished the sentence for her. "I know. I know. I forgot I was talking to Phoebe the Grand Speller of Glenfield."

"Apology accepted," she said smugly, but I was already halfway down the drive.

⁓ ⁓ ⁓

I took my usual seat next to Sam in the back row of Mr. Keefer's science class, where it was safe. Mr. Keefer was famous for being accident-prone—a dangerous thing for a science teacher to be. Those students who dared sit in the front row always ran the risk of being exposed to fire or extremely smelly chemical reactions.

Mr. Keefer was at the front of the room, trying to set up a film projector. All the other teachers at Glenfield Middle School used VCRs when they showed us movies, but Mr. Keefer stuck with the old film projector. It was rickety and usually had smoke coming out of it by the time the film was over. It was an accident waiting to happen—like Mr. Keefer himself.

I leaned Phoebe's cardboard tube against the back wall. Mr. Keefer stepped up to his podium at the front of the room.

"What's that?" Sam whispered, nodding at the tube while Mr. Keefer began to take roll. "Some kind of new invention?"

"It's the poster for the cafeteria," I whispered back. "Phoebe put it in the cardboard tube to keep it from getting wrinkled. Can you help me put it up before lunch?"

Sam shook her head. "I checked in the office about that," she whispered. "We don't hang the poster ourselves. We just drop it off at the custodian's office, and Mr. Lumpkin puts it up."

"Cool," I whispered. "I can give it to him when he comes to put out today's fire."

After taking attendance, we listened to the morning announcements over the P. A. system. Then Mr. Keefer rolled the projector into place. We were all a bit on edge. The last time he'd shown us a film, he'd gotten his tie caught in the reels and nearly strangled himself. If Mitch Reynolds hadn't found the scissors in Mr. Keefer's top drawer, who knows what might have happened. We all held our breath while Mr. Keefer flipped the switch on the old projector. It clattered into action, and circled numbers counted down to start the movie.

We'd been studying ecosystems. This was one of those nature films where lions chase antelope in slow motion. It was hard to pay attention. We all were watching the projector, waiting for it to explode.

Sometimes I'd look up at the film when the music (which sounded like it was being played underwater) got dramatic. I'd see a huge lion lope out of the brush in slow motion—its shoulder muscles rippling—to scatter a herd of frightened antelope. A few minutes before class ended, the projector started to smell like smoke. The movie ended in the nick of time.

When the bell rang, Sam and I headed for Mr. Lumpkin's office with the banner.

"So what do we do next, campaign manager?" I asked Sam.

"Well," she said, "we're turning in the poster and we've already collected the signatures. The only other thing we *have* to do is show up for the debate."

"*Debate*?" I asked, suddenly panicked. "I have to debate?"

"Well, duh," Sam said. "Don't you remember going to last year's debate? Everyone in school had to be there."

"Oh, man," I groaned. "I forgot about that. I never paid attention to those things." We stopped in front of Mr. Lumpkin's door. I knocked.

"Well, you'd better hope no one else pays attention to the debates," Sam said, grinning. "Harriet is captain of the debate team. She'll make mincemeat out of you."

My social studies teacher let us out a little late, so I rushed to the cafeteria to get there before the line got too long. When I turned the corner, I saw the line already had spilled out the cafeteria door and into the hallway. I sighed and walked to the end of the line.

I was nearly to the cafeteria door when Jesse Ingraffia came walking out. When he saw me, he grinned. "Nice poster, Willie," he said and headed down the hall.

"Thanks," I called after him. *Cool!* I thought. Phoebe must have done a good job. I couldn't wait to see it.

When the line moved forward again, I was in front of the cafeteria doorway. I craned my neck to see inside. Sam saw me and came rushing up.

"Just try to relax, Willie," she told me. "It's not that bad."

"I'm relaxed," I said, then my stomach clenched. "*What's* not that bad?"

"I'm sure Phoebe did her best."

"The poster?" I groaned. The line moved forward. I stood inside the cafeteria, looking at a giant poster with my name on it.

I'd thought it would be red, white, and blue—the way all campaign posters are. But Phoebe had other ideas. The letters were pink and powder blue. There were yellow flowers at each corner and a rainbow across the top. Each *I* was dotted with a big pink heart. It was the most feminine poster I'd ever seen.

I groaned. "It's supposed to be a campaign poster, not a baby shower announcement," I moaned. "How humiliating. My life is over."

"Relax," Sam said. "It's not hopeless. We'll turn it over and redo it. I'll go get some markers. You take the poster down and turn it over."

As I headed across the cafeteria toward Phoebe's poster, kids jeered and laughed. It was my fault. I should have taken the time to look at it before I gave it to Mr. Lumpkin.

"Hey, Willie," someone shouted, "can I borrow your lipstick?" Everyone burst into laughter. My face grew hot.

"He doesn't have lipstick," another voice yelled. "Can't you see he forgot his purse?" More laughter. I grabbed one corner of the poster and yanked it down.

"Don't take it down," someone behind me shouted. "It's just *darling.*"

Blushing deeply, I turned the poster around and stuck it back up. When Sam showed up with red and blue markers, we went to work redrawing the poster. I got hit on the back of the head by half a piece of garlic toast, but other than that, it went okay. But it was incredibly embarrassing.

When we were done, Sam and I stepped back and took a look at it. It was messy—the letters were all different sizes—but you could read it. At least it wasn't pink. I felt better.

Sam and I had just enough time to scarf down some food before our next class.

What's Felix Been Up To?

"I'm almost scared to open it," Sam said. We were standing by her locker after school. Neither of us had seen Felix all day. She grabbed her lock and started twisting the dial left and right. "I've received four notes from my 'Secrete' Admirer this week," she said. "He's driving me crazy. Whoever he is, I'd like to strangle him." She yanked on the lock, and it popped open.

"It's probably some quiet guy who sits in the back of one of your classes. He probably stares at the back of your head all period and draws hearts in his notebook," I told her. "All you need to do is find out who's flunking one of your classes. Piece of cake."

"You're still not off the hook," she told me. "I'm not completely convinced that you and Felix aren't behind this. It's just like something you guys would do." She stared at the unopened locker door and took a deep breath, getting up the nerve to open it.

"I've got to admit, I *wish* I'd thought of it," I told her. "But I'm as much in the dark as you are."

Sam pulled open her locker door. There, on top of her books and a rolled up sweatshirt, was a pink envelope. "No," she sighed. "Not again."

She picked up the envelope by one corner—like she was lifting a dead rat by its tail. She held it out in front of her and headed toward the trash can at the end of the row of lockers.

"You're not going to throw it away before you open it, are you?" I asked.

She turned back to look at me, still holding the envelope out in front of her. She raised one eyebrow. "Why are *you* so interested?" she asked. "Is it because you wrote something particularly clever this time?"

I laughed. "You're paranoid," I told her. "It's not from me. I just thought you should look at it. Maybe he signed it with his real name this time."

Sam sighed. "Okay," she said. "If you're so interested, *you* read it." She flicked her wrist, and the envelope sailed toward me and fluttered to the ground at my feet. I bent and picked it up.

Sam came back over and rummaged around in her locker, pretending not to be curious about what was in the envelope. I slipped my thumb under the flap and tore open the envelope. I felt like a movie star on Oscar night.

"Ladies and gentlemen," I announced, "this year's winner for Best Stalker in a Middle School goes to …"

I pulled out the letter and opened it. "The Secret Secreter."

"Funny, Willie," Sam said frostily. "You're absolutely hilarious. What's he say this time?"

"I thought you weren't interested," I teased her, grinning. "You were going to throw it away."

"Just tell me what it says, you big dope," Sam told me.

I cleared my throat and began reading like an actor in *Romeo and Juliet*. I even tried to fake an English accent.

> I like to watch you standing there.
> The way the wind blows thru your hare.

"There's that rabbit again," I said.

"Just read it," Sam told me.

I started over.

> I like to watch you standing there.
> The way the wind blows thru your hare.
> I also like to watch you walk.
> Someday I hope we'll get to talk.

"Until that day, I'll have to stalk," I added.

"It doesn't say that," Sam said, reading over my shoulder.

"I know, but it should."

"What's up?" a voice said behind us. Sam jumped. It was Felix. He looked like he was about to burst with excitement.

"Where have *you* been all day?" I asked him.

"Getting signatures on a ballot petition," he told me.

"You told me you'd already done that," I said, beginning to feel angry. "You mean I'm not on the ballot yet?" Felix had messed up some things in the past, but he'd promised I could trust him this time.

"*You're* on the ballot," Felix said. "I was getting signatures for the third candidate."

"*What?*"

"How could you *do* that?" Sam asked. "Willie is your friend!"

"Relax," Felix told us. "I know what I'm doing."

"Yeah," I said, "Stabbing me in the back is what you're doing."

"Oh, ye of little faith," Felix said. "I have been single-handedly winning you this election."

"Huh?"

"Can you beat Harriet Bink for class president?"

"Yeah," I said—even though I had some serious worries about the upcoming debate.

"Who *else* could you beat without even trying?" Felix asked me. "Who's the most unpopular student at Glenfield Middle School?"

I looked at Sam. She shrugged. I thought for a moment, then I knew the answer. "Leonard Grubb," I replied.

Felix grinned and nodded his head. I had no idea what was going on.

Sam's mouth dropped open. "You don't mean it," she said. "You're putting Leonard on the ballot?"

Felix nodded. He looked like he was going to burst with excitement. "I've got all the signatures I need already."

"Who'd want to sign a petition to put Leonard on the ballot?" I asked.

"Lots of people," Felix said. "At least once they knew it was to help you win the election."

"How in the world did you convince Leonard to run for president?" Sam asked.

Felix's glee disappeared. "Technically, Leonard doesn't know he's running for president."

"What?" I asked.

"You knucklehead," Sam said. "He's going to kill you when he finds out."

Felix swallowed. "I regret that I have but one life to give to Willie's election campaign," he said.

"You can't do this," I told him. "You can't railroad someone that way. Especially not someone as homicidal as Crusher Grubb."

"Too late," Felix said.

"What?"

"He's already been railroaded," Felix said. "That particular train has left the station. He's on Amtrak headed to Cedarville."

"You mean ..."

"I already turned in the petition. He's officially on the ballot."

"*Noooooo!*" I said, falling to my knees. "He's going to kill all three of us when he finds out." I glared up at Felix. "Make that *two* of us," I said, getting back to my feet. "One of us will already be dead." I reached for Felix's throat. He backed away.

"Dude," he said, "I was only thinking of you. I wanted to make sure you didn't lose the election."

"Instead, I'm going to lose most of my teeth," I said. "Some plan!"

"I'll talk to him," Felix promised, trying to calm me down. "I'll tell him what I did. We're on pretty good terms right now because I got him an A in science lab. I think he even likes me a little. I'll convince him he should run for president."

"Fat chance."

"No," Felix promised. "We're like this." He held up crossed fingers. "I'll see him in Mr. Keefer's class tomorrow afternoon. I'll talk to him then. It'll be okay. Trust me."

"I wish you'd stop saying that," I told him.

"I have just one favor to ask," Sam said. "When Leonard kills you, can I have your telescope?"

Isn't That Kind of Cheating?

I really wanted to be president. I wanted it bad. I wanted my picture in the yearbook on the first page of the student section—all by itself. I wanted my name added to the plaque that hung in the school office. I wanted to be important.

And I was sure this would just be the beginning. Before I was done, I'd have statues and monuments named for me. I was going to leave my mark on the *world*, not just Glenfield Middle School. I was hot stuff, and the world was going to know it.

That night I got ready for bed and turned off the overhead light. I pulled down the covers and slid between the cold sheets. I was so caught up in thinking about the election that I almost forgot to read my Bible. When I remembered, I rolled over and reached for the lamp on my nightstand. My hand groped through empty space. The lamp was gone. I groaned. Dad had struck again!

I got up and turned on the overhead light again. I went back to my bed and flipped through my Bible to Philippians, trying to find my place. I saw the verses I'd underlined and read them again.

Do nothing out of selfish ambition or
vain conceit, but in humility consider others
better than yourselves. Each of you should
look not only to your own interests, but also
to the interests of others.

A nagging question got hold of me: Why was I *really* running for president? Was it just selfish ambition? Was I thinking of only my own interests? What if Harriet would make a better president?

I didn't want to think about all that just then. There would be time for thinking about my motives later. I read the next chapter of Philippians and turned off the light. But those words from chapter 2 kept running through my mind.

$$\sim\!\!\curlyeqprec\!\!\curlyeqsucc$$

"So what did your Secret Secreter leave for you today?" I asked Sam when she joined me by the flagpole the next day after school.

"Nothing," she said. Her brow furrowed. "It's the first time this week that I haven't found something in my locker after my last class. I hope nothing happened to him."

"What?" I said. "All week you've been complaining about this guy, and now you're disappointed that he didn't leave you a note?"

"It *is* kind of weird," she admitted. "It actually was a bit of a letdown to open my locker and not find something waiting for me."

"You're starting to sound like Felix," I told her. "Always wishing things were the way they aren't."

Sam tucked her hair behind her ears and looked down at the base of the flagpole. "I keep thinking that maybe I *did* something today," she said. "You know—maybe I said something mean to the guy or treated him rudely. I'd hate to think I hurt someone's feelings without knowing it."

"A couple of days ago you wanted to have the guy killed," I said. "Now you're worried you hurt his feelings? Do you notice an inconsistency here?"

"I was wrong, okay?" Sam said. "I admit it. It was kind of nice to have an admirer. I just hope I didn't do anything to insult him. I'll have to be more careful."

"I'm sure he just missed school today," I told her. "Or maybe he got out of class late. There are thousands of reasons why he may not have left a note today. I just can't believe you're not relieved."

"Where do you suppose Felix is?" Sam asked, obviously wanting to change the subject.

I shrugged. "I don't know. Maybe Leonard Grubb killed him when Felix told him he was on the ballot."

"You think Leonard chased him down in slow motion?" Sam joked. "Should we wait for Felix? Or do you think he caught a ride with someone?"

I glanced at my wristwatch—3:17. "Felix is never late," I said. "If he was coming, he'd be here already. Let's start walking." We headed across the front lawn and crossed the street.

"Hey," Felix called out, running behind us. He sprinted across the school lawn and paused to look both ways before jogging across the street. "Wait for me."

Sam and I stopped walking, and Felix sprinted to catch up to us. When he got to us, he bent and put his hands on his knees and tried to catch his breath.

"Why didn't you wait for me?" he gasped.

"We thought you'd been eaten by lions," I told him.

"Huh?"

"We thought Leonard Grubb had killed you when you told him you'd put his name on the ballot."

"Yeah," Sam said. "I was on my way over to your house so I could pick up my new telescope."

"I told you guys I'd take care of it," Felix said. "And I did. It's a done deal. Leonard agreed to run for president to help you get elected, Willie."

My mouth fell open. I couldn't believe it. Why in the world would a guy like Leonard Grubb want to help me get elected? It made no sense.

"How in the world did you do that?" I asked him. "Did you make some kind of deal with him?"

Suddenly Felix looked flustered. He glanced at Sam, then looked down at his shoes.

"It's okay," Felix said. "I took care of everything. It'll all work out in the end."

"What did you tell Leonard I'd do for him if he won me the election?"

Felix looked up at me. "Nothing," he said. "Nothing at all. You don't have to do a thing, Willie."

I put my hands on my hips and gave Felix the suspicious look Mom gives me when she thinks I'm up to something. Felix squirmed a little, but he didn't say anything.

"You promise I don't have to do anything for Leonard?" I asked again.

"Not a thing," Felix said. "Trust me."

Sam laughed. We all headed over to my house.

"Why don't I write a bunch of questions for the debate and turn them in?" Felix asked, flipping through the television channels with the remote control. The three of us were all sitting in my living room. "That way you'll know what some of the questions will be. It'll be a big advantage."

"Isn't that kind of cheating?" Sam asked.

"Nawww," Felix said. "It's perfectly legit. The rules say that any student can submit questions. I'm a student. Besides, Harriet is captain of the debate team. She has an unfair advantage."

"But Willie isn't supposed to know what the questions are before they're asked," Sam said. "That's the whole point of the debate."

"He won't really know," Felix said. "They might not choose any of my questions."

Sam's brow furrowed. She looked concerned. "I still say it's cheating," she said. "But let's leave it up to Willie." Sam looked at me with one eyebrow raised. I just sat there. "Well?" she asked.

I wasn't sure. I'd been listening to the two of them debate about the debate. The trouble was they *both* sounded right. Sure it might be kind of cheating, but it would be nice to know I'd be asked some questions I could actually answer. Besides it didn't really break any rules. And I wanted to win this election.

"How about you submit only one question?" I suggested. It seemed like a good compromise to me.

Sam sighed and shook her head. "One question is still cheating," she said. "How would you like it if Harriet Bink's friends did the same thing for her?"

"It's not cheating. It's being smart," Felix said. "And besides, Harriet Bink doesn't have any friends."

Sam glared at Felix, then at me. "That's it. I'm outta here," she said. "I'm not going to be a part of this." She stood up and headed out of the living room.

Felix shrugged. "She has no imagination," he said. We heard the front door close. "What question should I submit?"

"How about something about the cafeteria," I suggested. "Everyone is always complaining about the cafeteria."

"Too easy," Felix said. "She'll be expecting it. And there's nothing a class president can really do about the cafeteria anyway."

Felix flipped through a few more channels until he found a cartoon. Bugs Bunny was hurtling through space in a rocket ship.

"I've got it," Felix said. "How about a question about the canceled field trip? Everybody's mad that we're not going. It's the prefect question."

I nodded as I thought about it. "It's good," I said. "It has only one flaw."

"What's that?"

"I don't know how to answer it."

"That's good," Felix said.

"How is that good?"

"If *you* can't think of an answer off the top of your head, neither can Harriet," Felix reasoned. "She won't be ready with an answer. But you—*you* can go do some research. You can talk to the principal. *You'll* have all the information. It'll show your leadership ability."

"I'm not going to be able to talk the principal into letting us go on the field trip," I said.

"Of course not," Felix said. "You're just a kid. The important thing is to sound like you're a leader—to let everyone know that you talked to the principal about it. Think of how it will make you look. Everyone will think that you've got all the information at your fingertips, that you know what's what."

"You sure?" I asked.

"Trust me," he said. I wished he'd stop saying that.

"Okay," I said. "You turn in the question, and I'll make an appointment at the principal's office. I'll get all the information that I can."

Felix pointed the remote control at the television and pressed the button a few times before the channel finally changed. "Dude," he said, "there's something wrong with your remote."

"Not so loud," I told him. "My dad will hear."

That night in bed, I couldn't sleep after I read my Bible. I wanted to be president so badly I was willing to cheat. My conscience wouldn't let me off the hook.

It's not really breaking any rule, I told myself, *just sort of bending one.* I tried to convince myself that, even though I was cheating, it was for the best. Once I won the election, I'd be able to do so much good for everyone that no one would care about a silly rule I had bent along the way.

The verses in Philippians kept coming back to me. I'm not putting my interests first, I tried to convince myself. I'm thinking about what I can do for everyone else if I become class president.

Let's face it. I wasn't just cheating, I was cheating out of *selfish ambition*. I cared more about being president than I cared about being right!

It took me a long time to get to sleep that night.

Anyone for a Simple Popularity Contest?

The morning of the debate, I took my seat on the folding chair in the front of the auditorium full of students. I felt like my tie was strangling me. I thought I was probably the most nervous person on the face of the earth. Then I looked at Leonard Grubb, who was sitting next to me. He was glazed in sweat and shaking like a washing machine on the spin cycle. He was wearing torn jeans and a T-shirt. How in the world had Felix talked him into going through with this?

Harriet sat on the other side of Leonard. She looked cool and prim, in complete control. This was just another debate to her. I looked out at the sea of bored faces in front of me and swallowed hard.

Mr. Keefer, the moderator, came out on the stage. He was holding a stack of index cards. He introduced the three of us, explained the rules of the debate, and shuffled the index cards.

"Willie, you'll be the first to answer this question," he announced. He squinted down at the top index card. "What are you planning to do to make sure we have a field trip to the observatory?"

I couldn't believe my luck. I got Felix's question right off the bat. I took a deep breath and stepped up to the podium. I was ready. I'd done my homework. I gripped the sides of the podium and looked out at my audience. I tried to look presidential. I cleared my throat.

"I met with the principal yesterday about this very matter," I said importantly. "We had a long talk about the budget. Unfortunately, there is simply no money for this year's field trip. We had to spend the funds set aside for the field trip on new lockers for the girls' gym. I'm sorry to report that it simply can't be done. We don't have the necessary funding."

I paused at the podium for a moment longer, trying to look tall and responsible. Then I went and sat down on my folding chair next to Leonard Grubb. I felt good. I was relaxed now. I'd answered the question, and I'd even used words like *budget* and *funding*. I was a big shot. This debate was mine.

"Leonard?" Mr. Keefer asked. "Leonard?" Leonard Grubb just sat there, dazed by the lights shining down on him.

"Leonard," I whispered. "It's your turn to answer the question. Get up there."

Leonard looked terrified. I actually felt sorry for him. He stood up slowly and made his shaky way to the microphone. He just stood there. Mr. Keefer furrowed his brow and stroked his beard a few times. He waited a few more seconds to see if Leonard would say anything.

"Would you like me to repeat the question?" Mr. Keefer asked.

Leonard still looked dazed. "I guess so," Leonard said. He scratched the back of his neck.

"What are you planning to do to make sure we have a field trip to the observatory?" Mr. Keefer read from the index card.

There was a long silence, then Leonard said, "Who wants to go to a stupid conservatory anyway?"

An awkward silence descended on the auditorium. Harriet Bink cleared her throat, but Leonard stood at the microphone for a few more awkward seconds before he turned around and headed for the empty chair beside me. He looked like he'd just escaped a firing squad. I really felt sorry for him.

Leonard collapsed into the chair next to me. He looked like he might slide right off his seat into a sweating heap on the stage floor. Harriet strode to the microphone.

"It's an *observatory*, not a *conservatory*," I whispered to Leonard, trying to be helpful. He ignored me.

Harriet adjusted the microphone and began to speak in her monotonous voice. "This year the cafeteria began serving juice in cans instead of the paper cartons we used last year."

I stared at the back of her head. What in the world was Harriet talking about? Hadn't she heard the question?

"As a result," she continued, "we throw away approximately six pounds of aluminum each day."

I smiled to myself. I must have really rattled her with the fact that I'd met with the principal. She obviously was avoiding the question.

"If we separated out those cans," Harriet continued, "we could recycle them for approximately $27 each week. By the first week of December, we'd have enough money to pay for our trip to the observatory. We'd also have enough money left over for a pizza party at the mall on the way home."

It took me a minute to grasp what was going on. Suddenly I got this sinking feeling.

"I've already talked to MacIntyre Recycling," Harriet said. "They're willing to add us to their Thursday pickup route. Mr. Reynolds at Home Warehouse has graciously offered to donate a large recycling bin for us to put in the cafeteria. All we have to do is fill it with our juice cans."

I felt like I had a rock in my stomach. I felt the debate slipping through my fingers. She'd done it. Harriet had thought of a way to get us our field trip— and all the pizza we could eat to boot.

"We'll also have enough money to pay for a similar field trip near the end of the school year," Harriet continued. "I'd like to suggest we go to the water park, but that can be decided later by a vote." Harriet turned smartly and walked back to her seat without looking at Leonard or me. She sat down and folded her hands in her lap.

Way in the back of the auditorium someone clapped rhythmically. Others joined in. In a few seconds the auditorium was thundering with applause. People everywhere chanted, "HAR-RI-ET! HAR-RI-ET! HAR-RI-ET!" I felt a drop of sweat trickle down my back.

What's the matter with her? I fumed. *Doesn't she know this is just a popularity contest?*

After the debate, I sat through my morning classes in a daze. I met Sam in the school cafeteria. I looked at Harriet Bink's poster on the wall, then down at my bowl of red Jell-O. I've got to admit I was tempted.

"I tried to tell you," Sam said. "Harriet may not be much fun, but she's full of good ideas. Something like this was bound to happen."

"It's just not fair," I said. "I've been working for years to be popular. I've been inventing things, risking my neck to make this boring town a bit more interesting. And what happens? Just when I finally decide to cash in on my popularity, Harriet pulls a quick one."

I looked up and saw Felix threading his way through the cafeteria crowd. He looked like he was in a great mood. He set his tray down on the table across from me and slid into his seat. He bowed his head and said a quick prayer. When he looked up, he was grinning again.

"Good old Harriet," Felix said, shaking his head. "She really saved the day this time. I could give her a big old wet one right on the lips." He pulled back the tab on his aluminum can of apple juice and held the can aloft in a toast to Harriet.

"I can't believe you said that," I sputtered. "I can't believe you just plopped down here and started talking about Harriet."

"Dude," Felix said, "everyone's talking about Harriet."

"This is not what I need to hear right now," I said loudly. "I'm losing an election to Harriet Bink. That's like scoring worse on an algebra test than Leonard Grubb." I glanced around quickly to make sure Leonard wasn't within hearing distance. Fortunately he was sitting alone, way on the other side of the cafeteria. But he seemed to be watching our table. I dropped my voice. "How can this possibly be happening?"

Sam was still watching Leonard Grubb. "Is it my imagination, or has he been less of a bully the last few weeks?" she asked.

"You're *not* losing the election," Felix said, ignoring Sam. "I said I could *kiss* Harriet—I didn't say I'd *vote* for her. You, I'd vote for." He raised his can again, toasting me this time. "But kissing you is out of the question," he added with a grin. "I want you to know that right now."

"Funny," I said coldly. "I'm laughing my head off."

"Leonard is still watching us," Sam said. We both ignored her.

"Look," I said to Felix, "you and I both know you'll vote for me because you're my friend. But what about all *those* guys?" I pointed at all the crowded cafeteria tables. "Who are *they* going to vote for?"

"You, of course," Felix said.

"I wouldn't be so sure," Sam chimed in.

I glared at her. "You really know how to make a guy feel good," I told her. "With friends like you, who needs Leonard Grubb?"

"Look, let's take a poll," Felix said confidently. "You'll see, Willie. You have nothing to worry about." He turned around in his seat and looked at the next table. "Yo, Brad!" he called. Brad Sargent looked up from his lunch. Brad sat next to me in English class. We'd worked on a couple of group projects together.

We were pretty good friends. "Who are you voting for?" Felix asked him. "Willie or Harriet?"

Brad snorted a laugh and looked over at me. "Stupid question," he said. Felix smiled.

I scooted my tray out of the way and leaned across the table. "This doesn't prove anything," I whispered to Felix. "Brad is my fr—"

"I'm voting for Harriet, of course," Brad said. "She's the bomb."

Felix's smile disappeared. My mouth dropped open. I stared at Brad, blinking. Brad took a sip from his aluminum juice can.

"I'm right here," I told him, tapping my chest. "At least you could *pretend* you're going to vote for me."

"No offense, Willie," Brad said. "But unless you buy us all pizza and a trip to the water park, you don't have a chance."

I groaned and put my head on the table. Sam patted me on the shoulder.

"Who asked your opinion?" Felix said to Brad.

"I can't believe this is happening," I mumbled, my head still resting on the cool table. "I'm less popular than Harriet Bink. My life is over."

"Nothing is over," Sam said. "There's still a week left before the election. A lot can happen in a week."

"Yeah," I hissed. "Harriet could figure out some way to build us a football stadium by selling our leftover pizza crusts to Bolivia."

"Calm down, Willie," Felix said. "It's true. Harriet saved our trip to the observatory, but that's a done deal. We're going on the trip, even if she doesn't get elected. Voting for her won't change that. All you've got to do is get people's attention so they remember how cool you are."

Maybe Felix was right. I lifted my head from the table and looked at him.

"A little publicity could turn the tide," Felix said.

"Maybe we could make a bunch of new posters," I said.

Sam shook her head. "You're only allowed to make one poster," she said. "That's the rule. People used to stick posters all over the walls, then they'd forget to take them down. Now you're only allowed one banner in the cafeteria."

An idea began to form in my mind. "What if we didn't *stick* the poster anywhere?" I asked.

"Right," Felix said. "What are you going to do— just hang it in midair?"

"Yeah," I said, sitting up straighter. "That's exactly what I'm going to do."

"Huh?" Felix said.

"You ever see one of those airplanes that drag long banners behind them?" I asked.

"You're going to rent a plane?" Felix asked. "Have you lost your mind?"

"Why would I *rent* a plane when my dad *owns* dozens of them?"

"Huh?"

"The remote control planes in my Dad's hobby shop," I said. "He flies them all the time."

"So you're going to have one fly a banner over the school," Sam said. "You know, that's a great idea. That would get everyone's attention."

In a few minutes, the three of us had formulated a plan.

"It's important that we all do our part," I told them. "I'll build the podium. Felix, you go by the hobby shop and get everything you need—I'll tell my dad you're coming. Sam, you need to come up with some kind of costume that will get some attention. I'll talk to Phoebe about a new banner."

I sat up straight in my chair and looked around at the noisy cafeteria tables. "By this time tomorrow," I vowed, "everyone in this cafeteria is going to be talking about *me*. No one's going to even remember what Harriet Bink did today."

Little did I know how right I'd be.

∽◡◡◡

"What do you mean, you need a new banner?" Phoebe asked, kneeling on her garage floor. She was bent over a new version of the Prince Charming mural she wanted to paint on her bedroom wall. "I just *made* you a banner."

I looked down at the large sheet of butcher paper spread out on the garage floor. Phoebe had nearly finished. There was no denying it—she was a born artist. I studied Prince Charming's face. With the pointed beard, it was hard to tell it was supposed to be me. Actually, I looked pretty good with a beard.

"Well, the poster you made before is more of a Jell-O target at this point," I admitted. "What I need now is something different. This election is getting out of hand. I'm in big trouble, so I'm staging a publicity stunt tomorrow at lunch. I need a long, thin banner. It should be light and streamlined."

Phoebe looked up from her work. "No problem, Willie," Phoebe said. "You cut it to the size you want, and I'll paint it. What should it say?"

"I'm not sure," I told her. "It's got to be easy to read from a distance. I think *WILLIE PLUMMET FOR CLASS PRESIDENT!* should be okay."

Phoebe nodded.

"No dumb little hearts this time," I told her. "No pink. No rainbows. Just red and blue letters."

"Okay," Phoebe said, obviously a little hurt.

"And don't put it in a tube this time," I told her. "I want to see it before I take it. I don't want any surprises this time."

"*Okay,*" Phoebe said. It was clear she was getting ticked. "But it'll cost you a goatee."

"Huh?"

"On my mural," Phoebe explained, pointing at Prince Charming with her paintbrush. "If you want me to paint another banner, I get to paint your face on my mural—*without* the goatee."

"This isn't fair," I sputtered. "You're taking advantage of my predicament."

"I get to shave Prince Charming or it's no banner," Phoebe repeated.

"Come on, Phoeb," I begged. "Give me a break here. If anyone sees this mural, I'll be a laughingstock. People will start bowing to me. They'll call me the student formerly known as Prince."

"No one's going to see it," Phoebe insisted. "No one ever comes into my room. That's my offer. Take it or leave it."

"Okay! Okay!" I said, exasperated. "But you've got to *promise* me you won't let any of your little friends in your room as long as that mural is on your wall."

Phoebe looked down at Prince Charming's face. "Okay," she said, holding out her paint-spattered hand for me to shake. "You've got yourself a deal."

I shook her hand. She handed me a pair of scissors. I knelt down and started cutting the butcher paper.

That night I went out into the garage to build the platform I would stand on tomorrow to make my speech. I connected some orange crates I'd gotten from the grocery store, then started working on the railing.

I looked all over the garage for Dad's electric saw. I couldn't find it anywhere. Without the saw, I'd have to use the handsaw. It would take me all night. I walked back inside the house and found Mom in the kitchen.

"Have you seen Dad's electric saw?" I asked her. I didn't really think she'd know; Mom never used Dad's power tools.

"As a matter of fact I saw it about an hour ago," she told me.

"Really?" I asked. "Where?"

"Under your dad's arm when he left for his electronics class," she told me. "He said it was making a funny noise."

9

Are You Sure That Isn't Latin?

My doorbell rang at 7:30 A.M., right on the dot. I grabbed my backpack and ran to the front door. My arm ached from using the handsaw the night before.

I opened the door, expecting to find Sam and Felix, but it was just Sam. She was wearing a dress—a pink frilly one at that! She had a plump grocery bag tucked under one arm. I stared at her, my mouth hanging open. Sam never wore dresses to school—let alone a fancy one like the one she had on now.

"You look a little tired," Sam said.

"You look a little weird," I told her.

"What do you mean?"

"You're wearing a dress," I said.

"No, duh," Sam said. "What was your first clue?"

"You never wear a dress," I told her.

"I wear a dress sometimes."

"Like when?" I asked. "The last time I saw you in a dress was at your aunt's wedding."

Sam crossed her arms and scowled at me. "I just felt like wearing a dress today," she said. "Get off my case."

"It just seems strange, that's all," I said. "Did you bring the costume?"

"Right here," Sam said, patting the grocery bag under her arm.

"Where's Felix? I thought we were going to check out Phoebe's banner together."

"He headed straight to school so he could test-fly the plane before anyone got there. Where's the podium?" Sam asked.

"Orville drove me to school before breakfast. We dropped it off on the playground. It's hidden behind the big maple tree. It's under a tarp. I don't think anyone will notice it before morning break."

I slung my backpack over one shoulder and stepped out onto the porch. "Bye, Mom!" I called into the house. "I'm leaving." I pulled the door shut with my aching arm. Sam and I walked across Phoebe's damp front lawn.

Sam in a dress. I couldn't get over it. Then it hit me. "It's because of your Secret Secreter, isn't it?" I said, laughing. "You're wearing a dress because you haven't gotten any mushy notes for a while."

"I am not," she said. "I just wanted to do something different today. Just drop it."

Sam glared down at Phoebe's lawn as we walked. I knew I was right. We headed up the drive to Phoebe's front door. I couldn't help but grin.

"Just because I'm wearing a dress doesn't mean I won't break both your legs," Sam told me when we got to Phoebe's doorstep. "Wipe that dopey smile off your face or you'll be shopping for crutches."

I rang Phoebe's doorbell. As soon as I did, the automatic garage door began to open.

"I'm in here," Phoebe called. "Everything's ready."

As the garage door opened, I could see the concrete floor strewn with paper and art supplies. Then I saw Phoebe's feet, then her legs and torso. When her head finally came into view, she had a puzzled look on her face.

"Oh, it's you," Phoebe said to Sam. "I saw the dress and I didn't know who it could be. That's a very pretty dress."

Sam screwed her face into a scowl. "Don't you start," she said.

The banner was stretched out on the floor at Phoebe's feet.

WILLIE PLUMMET
for CLASS PRESIDENT
Sapient—Veracious—Venerable

"What's that gibberish at the end?" I sputtered. "Can't you get anything right? All I asked for was a simple 'Willie Plummet for Class President.' "

"There was room left over," Phoebe said, "so I added some more."

"Obviously," I said. "But what *is* it? Latin?"

"No, dummy," Phoebe said. "It's English. I used my thesaurus."

"That's not English," I said. "I speak English and I've never heard of any of those words."

"They mean that you're wise, honest, and respected," Phoebe explained, obviously disappointed with my reaction.

"Who's going to know that?" I asked. "It looks like the stuff at the bottom of the ingredients list on a can of chili."

"It does not," Phoebe insisted. "It makes you seem smart."

"Get me some scissors," I demanded.

"No way!" Phoebe said. "I spent a lot of time on this—you're not cutting it in half."

"Maybe she's right," Sam said. "It *is* kind of cool. People will definitely notice it. The teachers will probably love it. Let's leave it the way it is."

I groaned. "Okay," I said. "I suppose when you ask the girl who took 16th place in the state spelling bee championship to make you a banner, you should expect this kind of thing."

Phoebe put her hands on her hips and scowled at me.

"Roll it up," I told her. "We don't have much time."

When we got to the end of Miller Street, Felix was standing in the middle of the road, looking across the intersection at the school yard. He stuck his finger in his mouth and held it up in the air, testing the wind.

"What do you think, Felix?" I asked him when we were close enough that I didn't have to shout.

"This is the spot, dude," Felix told me. "From right here I can get it off the ground before the intersection, fly it over the fence, and circle the playground as many times as you want. It's a piece of cake." He shot his hand out in front of him like a plane lifting off a runway.

"You sure this is the best place?" I asked, looking across at the school yard. "From here you can't see the whole playground."

"Yeah, I'm sure," he said. "I practiced a couple of times before anyone was around. It was easy. And Sam will be on the walkie-talkie to give me directions. All I have to do is stay away from the maple tree."

"You sure you can do it with the banner attached?"

"Positive."

"It'll add some weight and a lot of drag," I warned him. "You sure it'll clear the fence?"

"Trust me."

"I really wish you'd stop saying that," I told him. I handed him the rolled-up banner.

⌇⌇⌇

When Sam and I got to Mr. Keefer's class, he was busy setting up the rickety old projector again. After he took attendance and we listened to the morning announcements, he explained why we were seeing a movie.

"We're going to change things around a bit, now that our field trip to the observatory is back on," Mr. Keefer said. There was a smattering of applause for the field trip. "In the weeks ahead, we're going to do some work in astronomy to help prepare for what we'll see in Cedarville."

The film lasted all period, but I paid no attention. My nerves about the publicity stunt we were about to pull and my fears about the possible explosion of the smoking film projector left me without a clue as to what was going on in the movie.

When Mr. Keefer finally switched off the projector at the end of the period, you could almost hear the class sigh in relief that we'd made it through without a fire, a tie strangulation, or any other disaster. Mr. Keefer put the film back into its canister and dismissed the class.

Mr. Keefer followed Sam and me out of the room, rolling the projector on its cart. He seemed happy to have gotten through the class without one of his usual calamities.

"What did you think of today's film, Willie?" he asked happily.

I didn't know what to say. I hadn't watched a minute of the movie. "Say," I asked him, trying to change the subject, "did you remember to rewind the film?"

Mr. Keefer's smile suddenly vanished. One small mistake had flawed his otherwise perfect class.

"I'll have to do that when I get to the A.V. room," he said with a sigh.

By morning break, our publicity stunt was all set. Sam was with me, monitoring the walkie-talkie. Felix was outside on the street, getting the plane ready. I slipped into the bathroom to put on my costume—a white beard and an Uncle Sam top hat. I could hear kids' footsteps, heading out to the school yard. I looked at my reflection in the mirror over the sink and suddenly felt like an idiot.

Unlike my portrait in Phoebe's painting, I looked like a dork in this beard.

"You can't go through with this," I told my reflection. "You look like a sap. You'll be a laughingstock."

But as I heard the voices of the kids passing by, all I could think of was the debate and the sound of the whole auditorium chanting Harriet Bink's name. I had to do something to get myself noticed or I'd be forever remembered as the guy who took a pounding from Harriet Bink. It was time to give myself a pep talk. I leaned over the sink and looked myself in the eye.

"It's going to be okay," I told my reflection. "They're going to love it. You're going to blow them away. Today they'll be chanting *your* name."

I checked my beard in the mirror one last time, took a deep breath, and pulled open the bathroom door. When I stepped outside, Sam was waiting.

"Felix is ready," she told me, holding up the walkie-talkie. "All he needs is the signal."

"How about the podium?"

"I checked," she told me. "It's right smack in the middle of the school yard where you wanted it."

Sam and I walked toward the double doors that led out to the school yard.

"I feel like a sap," I told her.

"You look great," she told me. "This is going to be fun. Willie Plummet is no sap."

I pushed open the doors and strode out onto the playground. Some kids were milling around my platform, obviously wondering what it was for.

I took another deep breath and walked toward my podium. As I did, the playground fell silent. Everyone watched me. I felt myself blush. I wanted to turn and run back inside, but I forced myself to keep going. If I was going to get elected, I had to get some publicity—and that's definitely what I was getting now.

When I got to the platform, everyone backed away. I stepped up to the podium and turned to look at the crowd that had gathered. All the basketball and tetherball games had stopped. Everyone pushed closer to see what I was going to do.

I looked down at Sam. She smiled and nodded, trying to look encouraging. I swallowed hard.

"Ladies and gentlemen," I croaked, "may I have your attention please?"

There were a few seconds of awkward silence— I had their undivided attention. Hundreds of faces stared up at me. Even a few teachers had joined the back of the crowd. Behind me and off to the side, I heard the faint drone of a model airplane engine.

"As you know, I am running for a very special office at our school." I nodded at Sam, and she spoke into the walkie-talkie. Instantly, the drone of the airplane engine grew louder behind me.

"I just want you all to know that I'd appreciate your support. I'm very qualified to hold this office and I hope ..." At that point the engine sputtered, then I heard a loud tearing noise. I stopped talking and glanced at the fence around the school yard. There, flapping in the breeze, was a large sheet of butcher paper caught on the top wires of the chain-link fence.

I swallowed hard and ran my finger along the inside of my collar. *Oh great*, I thought. *The banner came off. Now all they'll see is the plane flying over the playground.* I should have been so lucky.

I stood there frozen, looking out at hundreds of silent kids. Suddenly someone laughed. A couple of people in front of me pointed up to the sky. I turned around to see what they were looking at.

There, flying over the school yard, was my dad's red remote control airplane. It was dragging the remnants of my banner. Everyone was laughing now. But what was so funny about a model airplane? I squinted to read what was left of the banner.

It took a minute for the new message to register in my mind. Then I groaned.

"You're right, Willie," someone called out. "I can't think of anyone more qualified for *that* special office." The crowd laughed.

"You got my vote, Willie," someone else shouted. There was more loud laughter. I looked down at Sam. She was staring up at the banner with her mouth open.

"Get it out of here!" I shouted to her. She blinked at me like she'd just come out of a trance.

"The walkie-talkie," I shouted over the noise of the laughing crowd. "Tell Felix to get it out of here."

Sam lifted the walkie-talkie to her mouth. The noise of the plane changed pitch. I looked up and saw it bank into a sharp turn and head straight for the big maple tree.

"Up!" I shouted at Sam. "Up! It's going to hit the tree!" Sam shouted into the walkie-talkie.

The plane suddenly veered upward. It clipped the top leaves and looked like it was going to stall, but suddenly it zoomed ahead again—without the banner. The plane swooped over toward Miller Street and disappeared behind some rooftops.

I looked down at the crowd. They were still laughing and pointing—at the maple tree now. There, high in the tree's branches, flapping like a flag, was the remains of my banner: *WILLIE FOR CLASS SAP.*

"Willie for Sap!" the chanting began.

"Willie for Sap!"

"Willie for Sap!"

I looked up at the banner. It was at least 40 feet in the air. There was no way I was ever going to get it down.

10

How about Popcorn and a Hot Dog?

At lunch I found a table in the back of the cafeteria where I could sit with my back to everyone. I was hoping no one would notice me, but with my bright red hair, I'm hard to miss.

People slapped me on the back as they passed. "You're the biggest sap in Glenfield," they told me. "You'll win by a landslide."

I heard my name over and over again in the cafeteria chatter—always followed by laughter. My cafeteria poster had been updated by someone with a black marker.

WILLIE WIN?
Only if you vote!
PLUMMET FOR PRESIDENT
And we thought the maple tree
Was the biggest sap in school!

Sam and Felix sat across from me. No one said anything. I just sat there, moving my macaroni around on my plate with my fork. I wanted to crawl into a hole and die. How could my day get any worse?

"Heads up," Sam said suddenly. I glanced up from my plate, expecting to be hit by flying tapioca pudding. "It's Crusher Grubb," she whispered. "He's coming up behind you."

Leonard Grubb! Just what I needed to finish off this horrible morning! I felt like one of the antelope in Mr. Keefer's film. I imagined a lion pounding across the ground in slow motion behind me.

Felix's eyes grew large. He looked at me, then looked over my shoulder and shook his head urgently.

I suddenly felt a large, warm hand on my shoulder. I stiffened, ready to be pulled off my seat and punted across the cafeteria. I remembered the bug-eyed look of the antelope in the film. I sat up straight. Felix looked more frightened than I had ever seen him.

"Felix," Leonard Grubb's voice boomed behind me, "do you want me to put the platform back behind the maple tree where I got it?"

Felix looked at me, then looked at Sam like a frightened rabbit. "Yeah," he said to Leonard. "That would be fine."

"Okay, Felix," Leonard said. "I'll be seeing you around." The heavy hand lifted from my shoulder.

"See you, Willie," Leonard added. "Good-bye, Samantha."

I heard Leonard's footsteps fade behind me and let out the breath I'd been holding. Sam sat with her mouth open, watching Leonard cross the cafeteria. We both looked at Felix. He put on the dopey grin he always uses when he's trying to look innocent.

"What was *that* all about?" I asked.

"You mean Leonard was the one who set up Willie's platform this morning?" Sam asked incredulously.

Felix glanced around the cafeteria, as if looking for an escape route. "Yeah," he stammered. "I couldn't operate the plane *and* get the platform ready, so I got Leonard to help."

It was all too weird—Leonard Grubb helping us out. We were natural enemies! We were his prey! It was like seeing the lion rush out of the jungle to help one of the antelope free its hoof from the mud. It made no sense.

"First, you get him to run for president so I can beat him," I said. "Now you've got him helping out with my campaign. What's going on here?"

Felix's head bobbed back and forth, from Sam to me and back again—like he was watching a Ping-Pong tournament.

"How are you getting Leonard to do all this stuff?" Sam asked. "This is too bizarre for words."

"Trust me," Felix said.

"No way!" I shouted. "Every time you say that, I end up deeper in trouble. I want to know how you're getting Leonard Grubb to do this—and I want to know *now*!"

Felix looked at Sam and laughed nervously. He looked back at me. "It's actually quite funny when you think about it," he said.

"Tell us!" Sam demanded.

"You know," Felix said, placing his palms flat on the tabletop. "Someday, we'll all look back on this and laugh."

"Spill it," I told Felix. "What's going on here? Stop stalling."

"Well, Leonard Grubb was hoping I'd help him out with something, in exchange for his services."

"Yeah?" I said. "What?"

"Well, it turns out that Leonard is very interested in our little group," Felix said.

"Why?" Sam asked. She looked suspicious.

"Well, actually it's *one* member of our group he's interested in," Felix's voice cracked.

"Huh?" I said.

Felix looked at Sam and smiled nervously. "Well, Sam," he said, "Leonard is under the impression that you're going with him to the movies Saturday afternoon."

"*What*!?" Sam shouted.

"Meet your Secret Admirer," Felix said. "He's hoping that—"

Sam lunged at Felix and knocked him off his chair before he could finish the sentence.

I dashed around the table and pulled her off him. Brad Sargent and Mitch Reynolds ran over and helped me hold her back. She was thrashing and kicking. It was all the three of us could do to hold on to her—she was practically foaming at the mouth, she was so mad.

Sam was right. Even in a dress she could break somebody's legs!

"No way!" Sam shouted. "It's not going to happen. I'm *not* doing it!"

We were on our way home after school. We hadn't seen one another since lunch. It had been a bad day. All of us were feeling lousy.

"It'll be okay," Felix said. "I'll buy you all the popcorn you can eat. It's only a couple of hours."

"I'm not going to sit through some dumb movie with Leonard Grubb," Sam said. "This is all too humiliating for words."

"It's my life we're talking about here," Felix pleaded. "What's that compared with a little humiliation? If you don't meet Leonard at the movie, he'll kill me."

"Well, what did you expect?" I asked. "Telling Leonard that Sam would go to a movie with him was stupid in about 320 different ways."

"Stay out of this, Willie," Felix said.

"Gladly." We walked half a block in silence.

"I can't believe you knew this whole time that Leonard was my secret admirer and you didn't say anything," Sam said to Felix. "I even wore a *dress* today."

"You told me you didn't wear that for your secret admirer," I reminded her.

"Stay out of this, Willie," Sam said.

"Gladly." We walked another block in silence, then turned onto my street.

"Listen, Felix," Sam said. "You're going to find Leonard first thing tomorrow, and you're going to tell him I'm *not* going to the movies." Felix winced just thinking about it. "Then you're going to tell him that this was all your dumb idea and that I knew nothing about it."

"He'll kill me."

"If you don't tell him, *I'll* kill you," Sam warned. "Then when I don't show up at the movies on Saturday, Leonard will kill you again."

Felix walked, his hands deep in his pockets. "This is a tough one," he said. "I don't know what to do."

"You get killed once or you get killed twice," I told him. "You do the math."

"Stay out of this, Willie," Felix said.

"Gladly."

"I'm so mad, I could spit," Sam said.

That night in bed, I thought about all that had happened that day. I've had some lousy days in my time, but this was among the worst. What made it so bad was that I knew deep down I'd brought it all on myself. Everything had happened because of my selfish ambition. I'd gotten us all into this mess because I wanted to be president. I thought I was such hot stuff that I couldn't possibly lose. Then, when it looked like I might, I was willing to bend the rules. I thought I was so important that someday they'd build monuments to me. Instead, I was the school laughingstock.

What was worse, I knew I deserved it. Talk about selfish ambition! Talk about thinking you're more important than others! I felt so bad, I didn't even touch my Bible that night. I was too afraid it would fall open to the those underlined verses in Philippians. I wanted to pray about it, but I didn't know where to start. I closed my eyes, murmuring, "God, help me."

I bumped into Felix on his way to homeroom the next morning. He had bags under his eyes, like he hadn't got much sleep last night either. We stopped for a moment in the hallway. He was holding a small paper bag.

"How's it going, Felix?" I asked. "Are you going to go through with it? Are you going to tell Leonard?"

Felix sighed. "Yeah," he said. "I can't think of any way out of it. I've got to face the music." He looked down at the floor tiles and sighed. I wanted to say some encouraging or hopeful words, but I couldn't think of a thing.

"It'll be okay," I told him lamely. "It might not be as bad as you think."

"Are you kidding?" he said. "This is the worst day of my life. First, the trip to the observatory gets canceled again. Now I've got to tell Leonard Grubb that Sam wouldn't sit through a movie with him if he was the last bully on earth."

"What do you mean, the trip got canceled?" I asked. "I thought we were going to raise all the money we needed by recycling aluminum cans."

"You mean you didn't hear?" Felix said a bit more energetically. For some reason he enjoyed telling bad news. "Mr. Keefer set off the sprinklers in the A.V. room and all the TVs and VCRs were ruined."

"What?"

"He was rewinding a film in there, and the smoke set off the fire sprinklers. Everything in the room got drenched."

Rewinding a film? Fire sprinklers? I'd done it again! I felt like banging my head on the wall. "Oh no," I said. "It's all my fault. I'm the one who reminded him to rewind the film."

"Whatever," Felix said. He had enough worries without having to take on one of mine. "Anyway, the field trip is off again. The money we save from recycling is going to pay for new televisions and VCRs. Not that it matters to me. I probably won't live to see second period."

"He's not going to kill you," I said. "I'll see you at lunch."

"Actually, you won't," Felix told me, holding up the paper bag. "I'll keep a low profile until all this blows over—Leonard won't seek revenge in class, but I'll have to make myself scarce between classes. I'll call you tonight if I'm still alive."

I went to Mr. Keefer's class. When the morning announcements came over the classroom loudspeaker, the vice principal told everyone that the field trip was off again. Everyone groaned. It looked like it was going to be another one of those days. But Felix had worse problems than I did. I said a quick prayer for him. He still had to face Leonard Grubb.

"I've been racking my brain all morning," I told Sam at lunch. "There's got to be a way to pay for new VCRs and televisions, but I can't think of it. Maybe I'm not cut out to be president. Maybe Harriet *should* be elected. She already solved this problem once."

"There's got to be some solution," Sam said.

"If there is, it's beyond me," I admitted. "Harriet probably will come up with something."

Sam shook her head. "Harriet's very organized," Sam said. "She's good at working out details, but she doesn't have your imagination. If you two weren't running against each other, you'd make a really good team."

I watched Harriet carry her tray to a table where some other girls were sitting. She dusted off one of the seats with a paper napkin and sat down.

"Harriet Bink," I said, more to myself than to Sam. "Who'd have thought she'd be elected president?"

"The election isn't until tomorrow," Sam said. "Anything can happen."

"Not a chance," I said. "She's definitely going to win. They'll probably name the A.V. room after her because she found the money to replace all the equipment. All I have is a flag flying from the maple tree telling everyone I'm a sap. Face it—it's over."

"That's okay," Sam said. "It's just an election. It's really not that important. What if you do lose? You're still Willie Plummet!"

Sam was right, but I still felt sorry for myself. I watched Harriet at her table, talking to her friends. She sat up very straight in her chair and never smiled.

"You really think the two of us would make a good team?" I asked.

Sam nodded.

"I'm going over to talk to her," I said. "Maybe we can work something out."

For some reason I felt nervous walking over to Harriet's table. I didn't really know any of the girls sitting with her. I set my tray down in front of the empty chair next to Harriet. All of the girls stopped talking and stared at me.

"Willie Plummet," Harriet said. It occurred to me that we'd gone to the same schools for years and we'd never really talked to each other.

"Hi, Harriet," I said. "Is it okay if I sit here?"

"Certainly," she said.

I sat down and looked around at all the faces staring at me.

"Look, could we talk in private?"

Almost as if they were communicating telepathically, all the other girls picked up their trays and quietly moved to the far end of the table. Harriet and I were alone.

"Harriet," I said. "I hate to admit this, but you're good at a lot of things that I'm lousy at."

She didn't say anything.

"I'm pretty sure you're going to win the election tomorrow," I went on. "And you deserve to, but I've got a favor to ask."

Harriet still didn't say anything. She just sat and stared at me.

"Everyone wants the field trip to the observatory," I said. "Can't we work together? With my imagination and your ability as an organizer, I'm sure we can come up with some kind of plan."

Harriet didn't say anything. I was getting nowhere.

Then the cafeteria fell silent. I looked up and saw a furious Leonard Grubb stomp among the tables, carrying his tray. Felix obviously had broken the news to Leonard. I just hoped Leonard hadn't broken Felix.

Leonard headed for the most crowded table—the table right in the center of the cafeteria. His face was red. He gripped the sides of his tray as though he might break it over his knee. I had never seen him so mad.

Leonard chose a seat and headed straight for it. The only problem was, someone already was sitting in it.

Brad Sargent was quietly listening to his Walkman, bobbing his head to a tune only he could hear. He had no idea Leonard Grubb was standing behind him.

Leonard grabbed Brad by the back of his collar and yanked him up off his seat. The Walkman clattered to the floor, along with Brad's tray. Leonard shoved Brad to the ground and sat down. There was a quick shuffling of feet, and suddenly Leonard was alone at the table. He glared around the crowded cafeteria as if daring anyone to challenge him.

Brad picked up his tray and his Walkman and came over to where Harriet and I were sitting. It hardly mattered. Harriet clearly wasn't in the mood to talk.

Brad sat down across from me. He looked flushed with embarrassment. He slipped the headphones over his ears, tried the buttons on his Walkman, then sighed when they didn't work.

"Broken?" I asked. Brad pulled the headphones down around his neck and nodded dismally. "Here," I said, holding out my hand. "I'll take it to my dad. He's taking an electronics class at the college. He's always looking for things to fix."

Brad looked hopeful. He slipped off the headphones and pushed the Walkman across the table toward me. At least I'd get to help someone today.

∂∼∼

"He's on a rampage," I told Sam. We were at her locker after school. "Leonard is terrifying everyone. I've never seen him so mean."

"I know. I know," Sam said, pulling open her lock-er door. "I feel terrible. I feel like it's my fault because I wouldn't go see that stupid movie …" She stopped talking, and the color drained from her face. There, on top of the books in her locker, was a folded note.

She picked it up and held it for a moment before unfolding it. I read it over her shoulder.

Dear Samantha

    I'm sorry you don't like me. I just thought you were a really cool girl, but I should have known that a girl like you won't like a guy like me.
    I will stop bothering you, and I won't be mean to you or any of your friends.

                   Leonard Grubb

Sam sighed and slowly refolded the note. She slipped it into the back pocket of her jeans. I could tell she felt bad.

"Well, Felix will be glad to hear that Leonard won't be mean to him," I said, trying to look on the bright side.

"Yeah," Sam said. "That's good news. But whoev-er thought I'd end up feeling sorry for Leonard Grubb?"

11

President *Who?*

"Wil-lie!" Mom called up the stairs. "Phone for you." *It must be Felix*, I thought. I closed my Bible, rolled off the bed, and went downstairs.

I picked up the phone off the kitchen counter. "So you're still alive," I said. "That's probably the only good news I'll get today."

There were a few seconds of silence on the other end of the phone. I heard a throat clearing. "This is Harriet," the voice said. "Harriet Bink."

"Harriet?" I said. "What are you calling about?"

"I just wanted you to know it's all set."

"What's all set?"

"The electronics class at the college wants to fix the damaged televisions and video recorders."

"Really?"

"I just got off the phone with the teacher," she said. "The college is even willing to pay for the parts if we can deliver the broken equipment to them tomorrow afternoon. I understand you have a pickup truck at your disposal?"

Harriet was amazing. She'd done it again. The solution was right under my nose, but *she* was the one who noticed it—and *she* was the one who got everything arranged. "Yeah," I said. "My brother has a pickup truck. I'm sure we can get everything out to the college tomorrow after school."

"Excellent," she said. "I've already written something that can be read with tomorrow's homeroom announcements." She had thought of everything. That's why she deserved to be president. "I just needed to make sure you could get the truck, Willie," she said. "Thank you and good night."

"Harriet?"

"Yes?"

"Thanks, Harriet," I said. "You're the best."

I hung up the phone and went back upstairs. I lay down on my bed. Tomorrow was the election and I was sure to lose. If I'd had a chance, it was gone now that Harriet had saved the field trip a second time. But what was strange was that fact that I felt good.

I opened my Bible to those verses in Philippians and read them again. A few nights ago I'd been willing to cheat to be elected president. Now I didn't really care if I got elected. I knew that the verse was right: I shouldn't just look at my own interests. Jesus certainly wasn't thinking of His own interests when He went to the cross. That was the kind of caring He'd help me feel for other people.

First thing tomorrow morning, the whole school would hear how Harriet saved the observatory field trip. They'd probably carry her home from school on their shoulders. But that didn't bother me—I'd learned a lot since the day I'd decided to run for president.

Music started playing. I groaned and stretched. I rolled over and looked at my clock radio. Seven o'clock. It was nice to have it back.

After breakfast I went upstairs and banged on Orville's door. He opened it, still brushing his teeth. "Ruh ruh rooo ront?" he asked.

"Four o'clock today," I reminded him. "Meet me out front of the school. The televisions are pretty big, so we might have to make two trips."

"Rhy ooo aaa afff ooo elp?" he asked, toothpaste dribbling down his chin.

"Because Dad said you have to help," I reminded him. "That's why. Now go wipe your chin. You're disgusting."

Sam met me at the corner so we could walk to school together.

"Well, this is it," she said. "Today's the big day."

"Nah," I told her. "A week ago I would have said this was a big day. Now it doesn't seem so important."

"You can still win," Sam said.

"I'm not going to win," I told her. "And you'll find out why when you hear the morning announcements."

Sam looked at me as we walked in silence. She seemed to be trying to figure me out. I felt like I had to explain it to her.

"I'm honestly glad I'm going to lose," I told her. "Harriet will do a much better job than I would."

Mr. Keefer took roll, then we waited for the morning announcements to come over the loudspeaker. There was a buzz and a crackle, then a voice began to speak.

The voice reminded us that today was election day. Polling booths had been set up in the cafeteria and would be open until the end of fourth period. The results would be announced during sixth period.

"We also are happy to announce that the observatory trip is back on again for the eighth-graders," the voice said. "The advanced electronics class at Glenfield Community College has agreed to fix the damaged audio-visual equipment at no charge to the school. Many thanks to Willie Plummet for proposing this solution."

I sat up straight in my chair. I couldn't believe what I'd just heard. *My* solution? Sure I'd mentioned my dad's electronics class when I was sitting with Harriet, but it had never occurred to me that it was the solution to our problem.

I looked around the classroom. Everyone was staring at me—even Sam. "Wil-lie! Wil-lie!" someone started chanting. In a few seconds, everyone in the class was chanting my name.

At lunch I sat in the cafeteria with Sam and Felix. Felix and I sat watching the door. I was waiting for Harriet. Felix was waiting for Leonard Grubb.

There was a long line in front of the voting booths as people took their turns voting. Sam and I already had voted during morning break. Felix had spent most of his free time hiding in the boys' bathroom on the second floor. We'd shown him Leonard's note, but he was convinced it was a trick designed to make him let his guard down.

"It's going to be a close one," Sam said, looking at the line in front of the voting booths. "How do you feel?"

"I'm okay," I said. "I'm actually hoping Harriet wins. I even voted for her."

Sam looked at me like she was proud of me. "You're a good man, Willie Plummet," she told me.

"If you had any sense, you'd vote for Harriet too, Felix." I looked to my right where Felix had been sitting a few seconds ago. His seat was empty. "Where'd he go?" I asked Sam.

She pointed under the table. "Leonard must have made his entrance," she whispered. Sure enough, I felt Felix's trembling body brush against my leg.

"What's he doing?" Felix's muffled voice drifted up from under the table.

Leonard walked right by the rack of trays and the serving counter and made a beeline toward us.

"He's coming this way," I said. Felix's head bumped the underside of the table.

"Owww," he said.

"Please, please, please, please, please, don't let Leonard come over here," Sam prayed under her breath.

Instead of coming to us, Leonard turned like he was going to join the end of the line at the voting booths.

I leaned back and whispered under the table. "He's getting in line to vote."

Wrong again. Leonard grabbed the last kid in line by the back of the neck and flung him out of line. The next kid he shoved to one side. He worked his way down the line, shoving and hurling bodies, until every one in line scattered. Then Leonard walked up to the front table and got his ballot.

The cafeteria was silent. Felix peeked over the edge of the table and watched. Leonard disappeared into the voting booth and appeared a moment later.

"I guess he wanted to make sure he got at least one vote," Felix said before his head disappeared under the table again.

The cafeteria was still silent. Everyone watched Leonard. He looked around at all of us. "Okay," he shouted. "Back in line."

No one moved.

"Now!" he snarled.

There was a stampede of feet, and suddenly there was a line in front of the polling booths again—except now it was about twice as long.

Leonard stomped out of the cafeteria. He was gone for a few seconds before people started talking again.

Felix was suddenly sitting beside me again. "What was *that* all about?" he asked.

"Everybody gets a vote," Sam said. "That's how the system works."

Then Harriet came through the door and got a tray from the rack. I went over and joined her in line.

"Harriet," I said, "that wasn't my idea."

She smiled faintly but didn't say anything.

"You thought up the whole thing," I told her. "And you made all the arrangements too. Why did you do it? Why did you tell them it was my idea? Don't you want to win the election?"

"I thought you told me about your dad's electronics class because you wanted me to make the arrangements," she said. "I thought it was your idea."

I studied her face. "No, you didn't," I said. "This is all your idea, and you know it. But you're giving me the credit. The least you can do is tell me why."

She looked at me and smiled again. She was kind of pretty when she smiled. "I want to win the election," she told me. "But I only want to win it fair and square. I want people to be able to choose who they think is best. I want everyone to remember that you're not a sap—that you're Willie Plummet."

I grinned at her. I couldn't help it. Harriet was all right. "Thank you, Harriet," I told her and held out my hand for her to shake. "May the best man win."

"Or woman," she corrected me.

I headed into my sixth period class and took a seat at the back. I felt butterflies in my stomach. When I arrived at school that morning, I thought I had absolutely no chance of being elected president, but a lot had changed since first period. I was in the race again, and it could go either way. Deep down I was still hoping it would go Harriet's way. I couldn't deny that she deserved it.

I thought about those verses in Philippians again: "Each of you should look not only to your own interests, but also to the interests of others." I looked at the other kids in my class. Some were leaning forward in their seats, taking notes. Others were drawing bored doodles in their notebooks. If I had these kids' interests in mind and not my own, who would I want to be president? It was obvious—Harriet.

Mrs. Clemmons, my math teacher, was up at the blackboard, showing the class something about exponents when the classroom loudspeaker finally began to buzz. I wiped my damp palms on my jeans.

"Please excuse this interruption," a woman's voice said. "The votes have been counted, and we are ready to announce the results of today's election."

Mrs. Clemmons put down her chalk. Everyone turned to look at the loudspeaker in the corner.

"Robert Wilson has been elected class treasurer," the voice said. A few of Robert's friends at the front of the class clapped. "Maria Vasquez has been elected to the social board," the voice continued. "And Tim Schulmann was elected vice president."

I held my breath. There was only one office left.

"I'm told that the election for president was especially close this year, but the winner of that office is …" the voice stopped in mid-sentence.

We heard the sound of a palm covering the microphone, then a muffled voice that asked, "Are you *sure*?" There was another pause. "*Really*?" the muffled voice said. There was another pause, then a stunned voice announced clearly, "The new class president is Leonard Grubb."

I was stunned. I sat blinking at the loudspeaker for a few seconds after the announcements were over. *Leonard Grubb*? How had that happened?

12

What Are *You* Smiling At?

"You can't blame *me* for this," Felix said. "How did I know he'd get elected? Putting Leonard on the ballot was a good idea at the time."

Sam, Felix, and I were standing in front of school with the damaged televisions and VCRs, waiting for Orville to show up with his pickup.

"Actually, you should blame Sam," Felix said. "It's more her fault."

"What?" Sam said. "How is it my fault?"

"If you hadn't broken up with Leonard, he wouldn't have gone on a rampage," Felix explained. "And if he hadn't gone on a rampage, no one would have been scared of voting against him."

"Broken up?" Sam sputtered. "What do you mean, I *broke up* with Leonard Grubb. I never had anything to do with Leonard. You're the one who told him I'd go to a movie with him."

"Oh, so it's my fault, is it?" Felix asked.

"Yes, it's your fault, you, you, ..." Sam shouted. "You and your stupid schemes. Trying to fix me up with Crusher Grubb. Now you've made Glenfield's biggest bully our class president."

"All you had to do was go to a stupid movie," Felix said. "No one asked you to marry the guy."

"What are *you* smiling at?" Sam asked me suddenly.

"I don't know," I said. "I guess I'm kind of relieved that I'm not going to be president. And you've got to admit, the whole thing is pretty funny."

"Yeah," Sam said. "We'll all be laughing our heads off when Leonard arranges our field trip to the *conservatory.*"

Just then Orville pulled into the parking lot. We loaded up the equipment. Felix and I rode in the back with the televisions and VCRs. Sam rode up front with Orville.

"You can't expect me to believe you didn't want to be elected," Felix said when we were on our way home. "If you didn't want to be president, why did we go to all this trouble?"

It was dark now, and the two of us hugged our knees in the back of Orville's pickup, trying to stay warm. I was glad the whole thing was over. I couldn't help but smile.

"Part of me wanted to be president," I admitted. "But it was probably the wrong part."

"What do you mean?" Felix asked.

"Well, I wanted to be president because I thought it would be cool to be important," I told him. "I didn't really run because I'd be a good president. I ran because I wanted to see my name on posters and have everyone's respect. It was all selfish ambition." I held on as the pickup turned a corner. "Now I know that kind of stuff isn't important."

We turned onto my street. We'd pass my house in a minute, go down a few blocks to drop off Felix, then head over to Sam's house.

Felix nodded. "I think I get it," he said.

"I'll never get my face on Mount Rushmore," I said, "but Jesus is showing me how to think more about others than about myself, and that's a much better deal."

We were just about in front of my house when the truck skidded to a halt. Felix rolled over onto his side. He pushed himself back up again. "Hey, what's the big idea?" he yelled at the pickup's back window.

We heard the gears grinding, then we scooted backward a few yards. Through the back window, I could see Orville grinning over at Sam.

The pickup stopped in front of Phoebe's house. Sam rolled down her window. "Do you see what I see?" she called back to us.

I looked at Phoebe's house. "What?" I said. "What's the big deal? It's just Phoebe's ..."

Then I saw it. The curtains in Phoebe's bedroom were open, and her lights were on. Framed by her bedroom window and lit up like a billboard was a huge picture of me, about to kiss a girl's hand. I was wearing a small crown, and pink hearts floated in the air around my head. I groaned.

She'd promised me that she wouldn't let anyone come into her room to see the mural. But there I was, larger than life, for the whole neighborhood to see every night.

"Looks like you got your monument after all, Willie," Felix said. All I could do was laugh.

Check out Willie, Sam, and Felix's next adventure. Here's a sneak peek from *The Monopoly*.

Once Felix got home and changed into dry clothes, he wanted to head to the mall to buy a new fishing rod. The closest sporting goods store was in Cedarville, but one of the department stores at Glenfield Mall had a small section of sports equipment. Felix wanted to see if they had any rods. He was anxious to go after Bertha at the first opportunity.

We rode our bikes to the mall. The store had a few rods, but Felix insisted none of them was worthy of a mortal enemy like Bertha. It was too late in the day to find a ride to Cedarville, so we decided to hang out at the mall. I tried the new Zombie Attack II game at the arcade, but after 10 minutes I'd already lost two dollars in quarters. I decided to give it a rest.

"Let's see if the toy shop's still open," Sam suggested. "It would be nice to walk through it one last
time."

"Okay with me," I said. The three of us headed
toward the other end of the mall. We passed the
Happy Traveler Luggage Shop and Luigi's Pet Shop.

"Any of these stores could be next," Sam said,
shaking her head.

"What do you mean?" Felix asked.

"Any of these stores could go out of business like
that." Sam snapped her fingers. "Glenfield is such a
small town, most of these stores survive because
there's no competition. They have a monopoly."

"Not that stupid game again," Felix said. We were
passing Lorson's Bookstore now.

"Look," Sam said, "if they opened one of those
super bookstores out on the interstate—or even
another small bookstore somewhere in town—this
one would have a hard time surviving. Glenfield's not
big enough to support two bookstores."

Neither Felix nor I said anything. Although neither of us would admit it, Sam did seem to understand
business—at least if winning at Monopoly was any
indication. We knew better than to argue with her.

In a minute we arrived at the site of the toy shop.
It was already closed up and dark. The sign had been
removed from above the door. A sheet of blue paper
was taped to the glass door. I stepped closer to read it.

★ Coming Soon ★

hobby station

Models, Airplanes, Trains, and Items for all Your Hobby Needs

Hobby Station? For almost 20 years, Dad's store—Plummet's Hobbies—had been the only hobby shop in the tri-county area. We had the market cornered, as Sam would say.

"This is bad," Felix said. "This is very bad."

I cupped my hands and peered through the glass doors. All the shelves and counters were gone. So were all the displays and lights. Even the carpet was torn up.

"I was just talking, Willie," Sam said, flustered. "I'm probably wrong. I mean, I was talking about bookstores. I'm sure this town's big enough for two hobby shops."

I stepped back and read the sign on the door again. *Coming Soon—Hobby Station.* There wasn't enough room in Glenfield for two toy shops. Would there be enough room for two hobby shops?

"Dad!" I shouted. "Dad!" I ran through the front door of Plummet's Hobbies, pushing my bike with me. The handlebars got caught on the door frame, and I nearly fell over trying to wrestle them through. I was out of breath from pedaling so hard.

Dad came out from behind the counter. "Where's the fire?" he asked, smiling.

"The mall," I gasped.

Orville came out from the storeroom.

"The mall's on fire?" Dad asked, alarmed.

"No," I told him, still gasping for air. "I was just at the mall."

"And?"

"The toy shop's gone," I managed to say.

"I know," he said, shaking his head. "I heard. It's a shame."

"But that's not all," I said. I took a couple of quick breaths. Dad and Orville looked at me, waiting to hear what I had to say. I hated to be the one to tell them the news. "They're replacing the toy store with a hobby shop."

Dad suddenly looked pale. "Are you sure?" he asked.

I nodded. "There was a sign on the door."

Dad stared at me. I wasn't sure what he was thinking. He looked worried, suddenly older. After a moment he patted my head like he used to do when I was a little kid. "It's okay, son," he told me. "We'll be okay."

I stayed at the hobby shop the rest of the afternoon, just helping out and sweeping up. I guess I wanted to assure myself that everything was really okay. Each time I looked at Dad, I'd find him standing behind the cash register, staring out the front window.

My family owned the hobby shop, but we weren't rich. The shop made enough money for us to live on. Some years, when business was bad, we'd have to do without a lot of things. We'd cut corners and stay home instead of going on a vacation. Some Christmases we hadn't been able to afford many presents. And now that my sister, Amanda, was getting ready to go to college, I knew my parents were worried about money. The news about the hobby shop couldn't have come at a worse time.

That whole afternoon only about a dozen people came into the store, and only six or seven actually bought something. If even a third of our business went over to the hobby shop at the mall, it could mean the end of Plummet's Hobbies.